S0-AGQ-367

Something's happened to Dru!

Emily reached over and turned out the light. Not because Caro had requested it, but because there didn't seem to be anything else she could do. She wandered over to her bunk and sat down on the edge of it, clasping her hands in her lap. Her mind was filled with pictures: Dru playing Monopoly with Penny on the floor of the cabin; Dru hanging on to Donna's saddle for dear life; Dru lying on the ground, scared and hurt. And then she thought of Dru trudging silently back down the trail to Webster's in the rain, clutching Donna's reins. Dru was a sad person. Emily didn't really understand sad people—she'd never run into one before, at least not one who was almost her own age. What had made Dru so sad? Didn't any of the rest of her cabin mates care? Penny cared, and Marie did, too. Now Marie and Penny were driving through the night trying to find Dru.

But what if they *didn't* find her? What if Dru was in real danger? What if she'd fallen into the river or something? What if . . . ?

HAPPY TRAILS
by Virginia Vail

Illustrated by Daniel Bodé

Ms. Fitch
Read it. Love it. Return it.

Troll Associates

Library of Congress Cataloging-in-Publication Data

Vail, Virginia.
    Happy trails / by Virginia Vail; illustrated by Daniel Bode.
        p.   cm.—(Horse crazy ; #2)
    Summary: Thirteen-year-old Emily's joy at spending the summer at a
horse camp is clouded by the depressed behavior of an overweight
misfit in her cabin, who resists attempts to make her feel better
about herself and eventually disappears with no explanation.
    ISBN 0-8167-1627-7 (lib. bdg.)   ISBN 0-8167-1628-5 (pbk.)
    [1. Camps—Fiction. 2. Horsemanship—Fiction. 3. Horses—
Fiction. 4. Lost children—Fiction. 5. Self-confidence—Fiction.]
I. Bode, Daniel, ill. II. Title. III. Series: Vail, Virginia.
Horse crazy ; #2.
PZ7.V192Hap 1990
[Fic]—dc19   89-30584

A TROLL BOOK, published by Troll Associates,
Mahwah, NJ 07430

Copyright © 1990 by Troll Associates, Mahwah, New Jersey

All rights reserved. No part of this book may be used or
reproduced in any manner whatsoever without written
permission from the publisher.

Printed in the United States of America.

10 9 8 7 6 5 4 3 2 1

Chapter 1

"Shorten up on those reins, Emily!" Pam Webster called from the center of the training ring. "Keep your hands apart—that's it. Now put him into a nice, slow canter. Good! Lean forward a little more—remember to keep your weight off his back so he can jump freely. Now take him over the jump."

Emily Jordan's heart was in her mouth as Joker, the big palomino, sailed over the single bar. Even though the bar was less than a foot off the ground, it was Emily's very first jump, and she felt like National Velvet riding The Pie. Imagine—she'd only been at Webster's Country Horse Camp for a little over a week, and she was jumping already! She could hardly wait to write to her best friend, Judy Bradford, and tell her all about it. Judy would have been at Webster's, too, if she hadn't broken her leg two days before the girls were supposed to leave for

1

camp, and Emily had promised to write every single day so Judy wouldn't feel too lonely and bored.

"Great, Emily!" Pam shouted. "Now slow him down to a walk and bring him over to the rail. Danny, it's your turn. Slow and easy, that's the way . . . . "

As Danielle Franciscus, one of Emily's cabin mates in the Fillies' bunkhouse, guided her horse, Misty, toward the jump, Emily leaned down and patted Joker's gleaming, golden shoulder. Emily's gray eyes glowed with love under the velvet hard hat that covered her wavy brown hair.

"*You're* great, Joker," she whispered to the horse, and his ears flicked back and forth as though he understood every word. Emily was sure he really did. She still couldn't quite believe her luck at having been assigned the most beautiful horse in the world for six weeks. It was like a dream come true. "You'd make anybody look good," she added.

When Emily had arrived at Webster's, she'd been afraid she would be among the worst riders there. It would have been humiliating to be placed in the beginners' class with a lot of little Foals, the eight- to eleven-year-old campers, most of whom rode ponies. But Matt Webster, the owner of the camp, had decided that Emily was an intermediate rider. Every morning after breakfast, Emily, Danny, and Penny, another Filly, joined several of the Thoroughbreds for classes with Pam Webster, the Fillies' counselor,

2

in the training ring midway between the beginners' and advanced areas.

"Libby, this isn't a steeplechase! Slow down!"

Matt's voice rang out from the advanced riders' ring, and Emily craned her neck, trying to see what her friend Libby Dexter was doing. She caught a flash of reddish brown as Libby's horse, Foxy, easily cleared a jump that must have been at least three feet high. Libby was hunched over his neck, her bottom high in the air. Libby was the same age as Emily—thirteen—but she was much smaller, and she hoped she wouldn't grow or else she'd never be able to realize her dream of becoming a jockey.

Danny trotted up next to Emily, her dark eyes shining. "It's kind of like flying, isn't it?" she asked as she slowed Misty to a stop. "Wow! Just call me Velvet Brown!"

Emily grinned. "Velvet, meet Velvet!" Both girls were crazy about *National Velvet.* It was a bond between them.

Emily watched intently as Penny Marshall took Dr. Pepper over the jump. With her blond braids and serious blue eyes, Penny reminded Emily of Heidi.

"I didn't fall off!" Penny said happily as she joined Emily and Danny by the fence. "How's Dru doing? Can you see?"

Emily, Danny, and Penny turned their eyes to the beginners' ring. Drucilla Carpenter was Penny's best friend. Like Penny, she was twelve going on thirteen, but Dru was overweight, wore braces, and seemed to be scared to death of horses. Emily hadn't figured out why Dru had come to Webster's. If you were terrified of horses, it just didn't make sense to spend your summer at a horse camp.

"Hey, she's actually posting!" Danny cried. "A little uneven, but she's doing it!"

Emily wasn't paying much attention to the beginners' class. She was focusing on the advanced ring, where Caroline Lescaux on Dark Victory was cantering toward the jump. Caro looked like a model in one of those fancy riding magazines. Unlike most of the other campers at Webster's, who practically lived in jeans, Caro's riding clothes were absolute perfection—and *very* expensive, as she made sure everyone knew. Only last week she had lent Emily a pair of her European riding pants—but that was before Emily had refused to trade horses with her for the summer. Caro hadn't spoken to Emily since.

Still, Caro rode beautifully, and as Emily watched, the slender, blond girl and the big, muscular bay soared over the jump with inches to spare. Emily caught her breath. If only one day she'd be able to ride like that!

"Okay, gang, you did real well. I'm proud of all of you," Pam said, striding over to where Emily, Danny, Penny, and the other intermediate riders sat patiently on their mounts. "Cool down your horses and take off their tack. I'll see you later, at lunch up at the house. Don't forget, Fillies are on dish detail today." At Webster's, all the campers helped out with chores, as well as caring for their horses. Webster's wasn't like any other camp Emily had ever heard of—it was more like becoming part of a very big family whose life centered around horses, and she loved everything about it.

Well, maybe not *everything*. Everything except Caro Lescaux. Emily had never had an enemy in her whole life, but she had one now, all right. And she was pretty sure Caro knew who had put that big, ugly bug in her bunk the other night. It had been Libby's idea, but Emily had actually done the dirty work. It served Caro right after she'd tried to steal Joker away from Emily by lying to Matt Webster!

Pam beamed her wide, horsey smile at her young charges. "Fillies, we'll meet in the stable yard right after water sports. If any of you have questions about our overnight trail ride tomorrow, we'll talk about it then, okay?"

"I can hardly wait, can you?" Danny said as the girls rode toward the stable. "It'll be so much fun, riding our horses to Willoughby Falls and camping out all night! My dad took us camping last summer, but it wasn't all that great. We drove to this campsite where there were lots of cabins and dozens of people. We didn't even have a *tent*."

Penny spoke up shyly. "I'm a Girl Scout. I've been on a lot of camping trips with my troop, but I've never been horse camping before."

"Neither have I," Emily said. She looked up at the

bright blue, cloudless sky. "I only hope it doesn't rain. Pam says the weather's very changeable in the Adirondacks—one minute it's just perfect, and then it gets cold and miserable, just like that."

"It wouldn't *dare* rain on the Fillies' very first overnight camping trip!" Danny stated, grinning. "It's going to be beautiful, I just know it."

"Maybe it'll rain," Dru mumbled later that afternoon. She and Penny were sitting on the floor of the Fillies' cabin playing Monopoly during the rest period between lunch and water sports. She was winning, but she didn't look happy. Dru never looked happy, Emily observed with a sigh. She was sitting on her lower bunk, writing her daily letter to Judy. Danny and Lynda, another Filly, were writing letters, too. Libby had gone off somewhere with Chris Webster, Pam's younger brother, and Caro was visiting her Thoroughbred friends in the cabin next door.

"Bite your tongue!" Danny called over to Dru. "Emily and I already settled it. It is *not* going to rain on our overnight trail ride!"

"You never can tell," Dru answered gloomily as she collected two hundred dollars and passed "Go."

Emily suddenly knew who Dru reminded her of—Eeyore in *Winnie the Pooh*. An image flashed through her mind of the sad gray donkey with Dru's face, braces and all, and it was all she could do to keep from giggling.

7

"Don't worry, Dru," Lynda said. "If it does rain, they'll just reschedule the ride for another day, and we'll probably have an extra class in the indoor ring instead." Lynda, like Libby, was an old-timer at Webster's. They had been coming to the camp for years, so they knew all the routines.

Dru mumbled something that no one but Penny could hear.

"Huh?" Lynda asked, sticking her head out over the foot of her bunk.

"She says she hopes it *does* rain," Penny translated. "She doesn't want to go. Nuts! I'm back in jail again!"

"Why not?" Emily found it hard to believe that even Eeyore—whoops, Dru—wouldn't want to do something that promised to be so exciting and such wonderful fun. Emily supposed it was because Dru was still scared of Donna, the plump little strawberry roan mare she'd been assigned for the summer. Or maybe she was afraid that since she wasn't as good a rider as the other Fillies, the rest of the girls would make fun of her. Caro probably would, Emily knew, but not the others. Remembering Dru's passion for sweets, she said, "I bet we'll be taking lots of marshmallows, Dru, for toasting over the campfire. And chocolate bars and graham crackers, for s'mores. You wouldn't want to miss that, would you?"

"I just don't want to go, that's all." Dru heaved

a long sigh. "I don't want to play anymore, Penny. I have to write to Mom and Dad."

Penny shrugged. "Okay with me. I'm just about bankrupt anyway." The two girls gathered together their play money and game pieces, and Dru put everything neatly away.

"How about going for a walk?" Penny suggested. "There's time to go see the sheep and the lambs before water sports. You could write to your folks after supper."

But Dru shook her head. "No, I want to write to them now. You go ahead if you want to."

"I'll go with you, Penny," Emily said, folding up her letter to Judy and putting it into the envelope. She quickly wrote Judy's address on the front and stuck on a stamp, then picked up the postcard she'd written to her parents and her brother, Eric. "Could we stop by the house on the way, so I can leave these for Marie to mail?" Marie Webster was Matt's wife. She ran the camp store, cooked delicious meals with the campers' help, and made sure that everyone's mail was put into the postman's hands when he came by each afternoon. She was a good rider, too—Emily had seen her on Queenie, her pure white mare. Marie and Matt often rode together after supper and before the evening's activities began.

Penny gave Emily a shy smile. "Okay. I'd really like to see those little lambs up close." She turned to her friend. "Dru, you sure you don't want to come?"

Dru said nothing, just shook her head again as she scribbled away.

"Penny, what's wrong with Dru?" Emily asked. She and Penny were following the grassy path that led to the sheep pasture. The sun was beating down on their bare heads, birds were singing in the trees, and the air smelled sweetly of warm grass and pine. *How could you possibly feel sad on a day like this?* Emily wondered.

"I'm not exactly sure," Penny replied, frowning a little and playing with one blond pigtail. "Dru doesn't talk much."

"Yes, I know. But she talks to you more than anybody else. I guess she's pretty homesick, right?"

"That's part of it, but I don't think that's the only thing bothering her. She really *is* scared of horses, you know."

"Then why did she ever come to Webster's?" Emily asked. "I've been trying to figure it out for over a week now. Did her parents *make* her come?"

"I think they did, kind of, only I don't know why they chose a horse camp. Dru has two older sisters and an older brother, and they're all at camp this summer. I get the feeling that maybe there's something wrong with her parents. I think she's worried about them, but she won't say why."

Emily bent down and pulled a stalk of grass, pop-

10

ping the end into her mouth and savoring its fresh juiciness. No wonder horses liked to eat grass—it was really delicious! "I don't mean to be nosy," she said, "though I guess it looks that way. But I can't help worrying about Dru. Maybe it's because before I got here, I was afraid *I'd* be miserable and unhappy without my best friend. Judy was supposed to come, too, but she broke her leg."

"How'd she do that?" Penny wanted to know, so Emily told her all about Judy falling out of a tree while rescuing her kitten, Sprinkles, and Penny told Emily all about her cat who'd just had kittens. By the time they reached the sheep pasture, the subject of Dru had been forgotten for the moment.

"Aren't they the cutest things you ever saw?" Penny asked, gazing in delight at the lambs frisking on spindly black legs around their placid mothers.

"I'd love to have a pet lamb," Emily said. "The only trouble is, they grow up to be big, dumb sheep!"

"I wonder if that's what our parents think about us when we're cute little babies," Penny said with a giggle. " 'They're adorable now, but wait till they grow up to be big, dumb kids!' "

Emily laughed, too. Penny really surprised her—she hadn't realized Penny had a sense of humor, probably because she was always hanging out with Dru. Spending a lot of time with Dru Carpenter wouldn't give you much to giggle about, that was for sure!

When the girls returned to the cabin just in time to change into their swimsuits, Emily had gotten to know Penny much better. But she still hadn't solved the mystery of Dru.

Chapter 2

The Fillies' bunkhouse was in turmoil the following morning as everyone started packing for the overnight trail ride, trying to fit their possessions into compact, tidy blanket rolls. All Fillies had been excused from the last hour of riding classes in order to prepare for the trip, because they were to leave right after lunch.

"Caro, believe me, you are *not* going to need your bathrobe, slippers, and another pair of riding pants," Lynda sighed. "And you won't need all that makeup, either. Nobody's going to see you except us and the horses, and I don't know about the horses, but *we* won't care if you're not wearing eye shadow first thing in the morning!"

"*I* care," Caro stated firmly. "And I *will* need my bathrobe and slippers. What if I have to go to the bathroom in the middle of the night?"

14

"What bathroom?" Libby asked. "We're going on a trail ride, not a trip to some fancy resort. If nature calls, you just crawl out of your tent and disappear into the woods. And we'll shower at the Falls in our bathing suits."

"Yes, Caro, you better just take the things Pam told us to take," Danny added. "Clean underwear, toothbrush and toothpaste, pajamas, socks, soap, hairbrush, and comb. We're only going to be gone one night—we don't have to carry a lot of extra junk with us."

"For your information, Danny, I don't consider a clean shirt and riding pants 'extra junk'!" Caro snapped. "*You* may be perfectly comfortable wearing the same clothes day after day, but *I'm* not." She scowled at the pile of clothing she'd assembled in the middle of her blanket. "I don't see why Warren couldn't just pick up all our stuff and take it to the campsite in the van. This *is* the twentieth century, and we're *not* Lewis and Clark setting out on an expedition."

Lynda finished tying up her blanket roll and said patiently, "Caro, the point of an overnight trail ride is that we carry everything ourselves—except for the food and tents and cooking equipment. That'll be on the pack horse that Chris leads. Besides, there's no road to Willoughby Falls that the van could drive on. It's very deep in the woods. We're roughing it, just us and the horses."

Emily had been trying to make a tidy bundle of

15

her belongings, but in spite of her efforts, every time she rolled them up in the blanket something fell out. She picked up her toothbrush and gave it a dirty look. "Will you *please* stay where you're supposed to be?"

"If you wrap all the little stuff in your underwear, it'll stay put," Penny said. "Here, I'll show you."

She tucked Emily's toothbrush, comb, and soap into a neat bundle surrounded by Emily's undies and wrapped the bundle in her pajamas, then rolled everything in the blanket.

"That's the way they taught us in Girl Scouts," Penny said.

"Thanks, Penny," Emily said and smiled. Lowering her voice, she asked, "Is Dru all packed and ready to go?" From the looks of Dru, who was sitting on her bunk with her arms folded across her plump middle, she wasn't ready to go anywhere.

"Well, she's *packed,*" Penny replied.

"I don't feel very well. My stomach hurts," Dru said in a small voice. "I think I'd better go see Marie." Marie Webster was a registered nurse and ran the infirmary. "Maybe I'm coming down with something."

Caro sat back on her heels by her pile of belongings and gave Dru a withering look. "If you ask me, the only thing you're coming down with is those four muffins you ate for breakfast, on top of two helpings of scrambled eggs and a stack of pancakes," she said.

16

"Well, I *didn't* ask you!" Dru muttered. "I have to keep up my strength. I'm still growing."

"Yeah—sideways!" Caro retorted.

"Oh, stop it, you two!" Libby said. "What's the matter with you both? This is supposed to be *fun!* And it will be, if you'll just stop complaining."

Emily sighed. Libby was right—Caro and Dru could ruin the trail ride for everyone before they even started out. Maybe it was because of the heat. The day had dawned clear but hazy, and had been getting steadily hotter as the sun climbed higher in the sky. Emily's shirt was sticking to her back, and her soft brown waves were springier than usual because of the dampness. Dru had to be feeling the heat even more since she was—Emily thought "fat," then charitably changed it to "slightly overweight."

But the hot weather was no excuse for Caro. She was model-slim, and never seemed to perspire. No, Caro was just being mean. She was always teasing Dru about how much the younger girl ate. And that wasn't fair at all, because Caro ate a lot, too. It just didn't show on her.

"Well, I'm all packed," Danny said cheerfully, tossing her blanket roll on the floor. "Are we going to leave right after lunch? No swimming or anything?"

"Nope—we'll swim when we get to Willoughby Falls," Lynda said. "There's this terrific natural pool at the base of the falls, and it's all bubbly be-

17

cause of the water pouring into it. It's much nicer than swimming in the Winnepac."

"I've been to Niagara Falls," Caro said, struggling to wrap all her clothing and accessories in her blanket. "I'm sure Willoughby Falls can't compare with the majesty and power of Niagara."

"You're right," Lynda said. "But Willoughby Falls is very pretty. And Libby rode Foxy right into the pool last year—remember, Libby?"

Libby grinned. "Do I ever! He loved it as much as I did! Have you ever seen a horse swim? Well, they can. Maybe I'll do it again this year and show you."

"Cats can swim, too," Danny offered. "We took our cat with us when our family went camping, and my little brother threw him into the lake. We thought he'd drown, but he didn't. He swam like anything! He didn't like it much, though."

Caro wasn't interested in stories of swimming horses and cats. She was too busy trying to make a blanket roll.

"Would you like me to help you, Caro?" Penny suggested. "All you have to do is . . . "

Emily watched, fascinated, as Penny quickly turned Caro's mound of "necessities" into a tight bundle. Even Caro was impressed.

"Girl Scouts," Penny said matter-of-factly.

"Everybody ready?"

Pam Webster, seated on Firefly, a big, rangy bay,

18

surveyed her troops. Each Filly's blanket roll had been strapped to the back of her saddle, and the pack horse, an elderly pinto, was secured by a lead-line to Chris's hand. Chris was riding Buster, his roan gelding. Buster's ears flicked back and forth, as though he was listening to every word and taking notes.

"Ready!" all the Fillies shouted—except Dru, who, as usual, said nothing.

"Then let's go!"

Pam waved her arm like a general at the head of a battalion, and the Fillies followed where she led, down the path from the stables, through the pastures, and toward the tall, dark evergreens of the forest.

Emily's eyes were shining. She was going to spend an entire day and night with Joker, and not even Dru's glumness or Caro's nastiness could dim the excitement she felt. Her first overnight trail ride!

Libby and Foxy trotted up next to Emily. "This is gonna be absolutely *great*, Emily! You're gonna love it!"

Emily grinned back. "I know!"

Pam led the way down a narrow trail beneath low-hanging branches, calling over her shoulder, "Don't hold back a branch when you pass under it—it'll only swing back and knock the next rider out of the saddle. Just duck!"

Emily ducked. As she did, she noticed a little wedge-shaped brown insect on Joker's glossy neck.

19

She smacked it, and to her dismay saw a tiny splotch of blood.

"Yuck!" She quickly wiped her hand on her jeans. "What was that, anyway?" she asked Libby. "It wasn't a horsefly or a mosquito, but it was making a meal out of Joker!"

Libby shrugged. "I don't know what you call them, but they come out whenever it's hot and damp, like today. They don't seem to bother people much—just horses."

"I'd rather have them bite me than Joker," Emily said. She resolved to keep an eye out for the nasty little creatures so they wouldn't eat Joker alive. Joker was trying to protect himself as well—he was swishing his silvery tail back and forth like a flyswatter, and so were all the other horses.

Emily rubbed the back of her hand across her forehead. Perspiration was trickling down from under her black velvet hard hat, and she wished she could take it off. But it was an unbreakable rule at Webster's that you always wore your hard hat when you were riding. Emily was just glad that the campers didn't have to wear the protective chin harness except when they were jumping—she was sure she'd have itched like crazy from prickly heat.

The sky, which had been so clear and blue earlier in the day, had misted over, making it feel muggy and hotter. There didn't seem to be a single breeze stirring as the Fillies followed Pam deeper into the woods. The trail was much narrower now, with trees

20

and dense shrubbery on either side. Emily wondered how long it would be until they reached Willoughby Falls. The thought of plunging into fresh, cold water was immensely appealing.

Libby had fallen behind her now, since there wasn't any room on the trail to ride side by side. Dru was in front of her.

"I think it's going to rain," she heard Dru say to nobody in particular. "Maybe we ought to turn back."

Emily gritted her teeth, but kept her voice cheerful as she said, "Oh, I don't think so, Dru. Wait till we get to the falls. We'll all have a good swim and cool off."

"Keep your hands steady on the reins, girls," Pam called over her shoulder. "The trail's starting to go uphill, and there are a lot of rocks and roots. If your horse starts to stumble, you have to keep his head up so he doesn't get frightened."

"I'm going to fall off, I know I will!" Dru wailed.

Emily heard Penny's patient voice floating back from in front of Dru. "No, you won't. You're going to be just fine. Don't worry so much, Dru."

The trail did indeed go uphill, and then it went down and around and up again. It was a little cooler now and a light breeze had sprung up. Emily thought maybe they were getting close to the falls. She wasn't really in any hurry, though. This was the longest ride she'd ever taken on Joker, and she was loving every minute of it. Joker seemed to be enjoying it, too. His ears were pricked up all the time, except when Emily spoke to him. Then they flicked back—to hear her better, she was sure.

"Let's sing something," Lynda called. She and Dan, the dapple gray gelding she always rode, were last in line.

"Yeah! How about 'Green Grow the Rushes, Oh'?" Libby called back. "Everybody know that one?"

Everyone said they did, except Dru. "I don't know any camp songs," she said. "And if I did, I'd be afraid to sing, because it might scare Donna, and then I'd fall off."

"Give me a break!" Libby sighed. Then, loudly, so Dru could hear her, she added, "Webster's horses are used to singing. They *love* singing. I bet they even know all the words!"

"You'll learn it real fast," Emily put in. "It's a counting song, like 'The Twelve Days of Christmas.' You sing the same words over and over."

"I always get mixed up on 'The Twelve Days of Christmas,'" Dru said woefully. "I can never remember if it's 'six geese a-swimming' or 'six swans a-laying.'"

"Don't worry, there aren't any geese or swans in this one," Penny assured her. "Just listen. You'll catch on."

Lynda began singing at the top of her lungs:
"I'll sing you one, oh.
Green grow the rushes, oh!

22

What is your one, oh?

One is one and all alone and ever more shall be so."

The rest of the girls joined in, a little raggedly, but with lots of enthusiasm:

"I'll sing you two, oh.

Green grow the rushes, oh!

What is your two, oh?

Two, two the lily-white boys clothed all in green, oh.

One is one and all alone and ever more shall be so."

"Who are the lily-white boys?" Dru wanted to know. "And what's 'one'? This song doesn't make any sense."

"It doesn't have to make sense. It's just a nice song," Emily said. "Let's sing the rest of the verses."

They launched into the third verse:

"I'll sing you three, oh.

Green grow the rushes, oh!

What is your three, oh?

Three, three the rivals,

Two, two the lily-white boys clothed all in green, oh.

One is one and all alone and ever more shall be so."

23

"Who are the rivals? It doesn't . . . "
"I'll sing you four, oh.
  Green grow the rushes, oh!
  What is your four, oh? . . . "
And then Dru fell off.

Chapter 3

Emily couldn't believe her eyes. One minute, Donna was plodding calmly along the trail with Dru on her back. The next, Donna was standing still, her saddle empty, looking down at Dru in a crumpled heap on the ground. Donna looked puzzled. So did Emily—and she was scared. Dru wasn't moving a muscle. She just lay there like a stuffed toy that some gigantic child had discarded.

Emily pulled Joker to an abrupt halt. Libby and Lynda, immediately behind her, stopped, too.

"What's the matter?" Lynda called.

"Holy cow!" Libby squawked, seeing Donna's empty saddle. "Where's Dru?"

Emily pointed. Libby and Lynda craned their necks and gasped in unison.

"Omigosh!" Lynda cried. "What happened to her?"

"I don't know," Emily replied shakily. "She was fine, and then I must have blinked or something, and when I looked again, she wasn't there."

Dru still didn't move, but her voice, faint and strained, drifted up to her worried bunkmates. "I fell off," she said. "I told you I would, and I did."

"I'll sing you five, oh.

Green grow the rushes, oh!

What is your five, oh?

Five for the symbols at your door . . . "

The rest of the Fillies, unaware that anything was wrong, were proceeding down the trail, singing cheerfully.

" . . . Three, three the rivals,

Two, two the lily-white boys clothed all in green, oh.

One is one and all alone and ever more shall be so!

I'll sing you six, oh . . . "

"*Pam!*" Libby hollered as loud as she could, but nobody heard.

" . . . Six for the six proud walkers,

Five for the symbols at your door . . . "

"I've got to get Pam," Lynda said, edging Dan around Foxy, Joker, and Donna on the narrow trail. "We're never supposed to get off our horses on a trail ride unless there's an emergency, but this is definitely an emergency, so I think you two better dismount and see if there's anything you can do for Dru. Don't move her, though—she might have broken bones or something," she added as she urged Dan into a brisk trot. "Pam will know what to do."

Emily swung down from Joker's back as Libby leaped out of Foxy's saddle and ran to Dru. Holding Joker's reins, Emily hurried over to Donna and gathered her reins, too, though Donna showed no signs of running away. The little strawberry roan was placidly munching on the leaves of a nearby shrub, occasionally casting mildly interested glances at her former rider.

"Well, at least she can talk," Emily said, "so she's not unconscious." But all sorts of terrible possibilities were running through her mind. What if Dru's tummyache had been the first symptom of some awful disease, and Dru had become really sick? What if she fainted because of the heat? What if Donna *had* been spooked by the singing, and in that moment when Emily hadn't been looking, she'd bucked or something? What if there had been something Emily could have done to prevent this from happening? Emily bit her lip, wishing there was something she could do to help.

Libby knelt next to Dru and gently removed her hard hat, wiping Dru's forehead with a bandanna she'd taken from her hip pocket. "What *happened*, Dru?" she asked anxiously. "Are you all right? Does anything hurt?"

"*Everything* hurts," Dru moaned. "I think it was those little brown bugs. I think one of them bit

Donna, and she got mad. That's when she threw me."

Emily frowned. Donna *threw* Dru? Calm, quiet Donna?

"I want to go back to camp," Dru mumbled. "And then I want to go *home!*"

"Take it easy, Dru," Libby said. "Lynda's going to get Pam, and she'll take care of everything. You just lie here and rest."

The singing had stopped. A moment later, Lynda returned with Pam. "Hey, Dru, what's happening?" Pam said, quickly dismounting and coming over to Dru. She dropped onto her knees and expertly ran her hands over Dru's back and legs. In spite of her usual friendly smile, Emily could tell that Pam was worried. "Can you move your legs?" Pam asked.

Dru lifted first one leg, then the other. "Yes. They're okay."

"What about your arms? Move your arms, Dru."

Dru did.

"Do you think you can sit up?"

Very slowly, Dru sat up.

"Super! How does your head feel? Did you bump your head on a rock or anything?"

"I—I don't think so. I was wearing my hard hat, like you told us to."

Pam breathed a sigh of relief, and so did Emily.

"How did it happen, Dru? Tell me about it."

"Well . . . " Dru blew her nose on Libby's bandanna. "I'm not really sure. All of a sudden, I just fell off."

"*Really*!" Caro sneered. Out of curiosity, she'd followed Pam to the scene of the accident, and now she was becoming impatient with the lack of drama. "You're the only person I ever knew who could fall off a horse who was *walking*!"

"Caro, cool it!" Pam ordered. She turned back to Dru. "If you're not really hurt—and I don't think you are—the best thing is to get back on your horse and keep going. We're only about fifteen minutes from Willoughby Falls. Listen—can't you hear the sound?"

Emily listened. There was a faint roar in the distance, like water falling over rocks.

"I don't want to go to Willoughby Falls," Dru moaned. "I just want to go back. I could have internal injuries. I have this pain in my stomach . . . ."

There was a long silence. Finally, Libby said, "Pam, maybe it wouldn't be a bad idea to take Dru back to the camp. Maybe Marie ought to take a look at her. I could take her back, so the rest of the Fillies could camp out tonight."

Suddenly Danny cried out, "Hey, we must be real close to the falls! I can feel drops of water!"

Pam sighed. "That's not from the falls, Danny. That's *rain*. It's starting to rain." She looked from Danny to Libby. "Libby, I can't let you take Dru back on your own. I'm in charge of this trail ride, and whatever happens is my responsibility. And if I take Dru back, you can't camp out without me."

"You could put me in charge, Pam," Chris offered. "I know the whole routine as well as you do."

"No way," Pam said firmly. "You know what Mom and Dad say—there has to be a senior counselor with every group, and you're not a senior counselor."

"Besides, it's raining," Dru said triumphantly. "And it's probably going to rain a lot harder. I don't care who takes me back. I'll go back all by myself. But I don't want to camp out in the rain! I'll walk back if I have to, but I'm not going to get back up on Donna. I'd rather lie here until I *die*!"

"Dru, you're not going to die," Penny said softly. "And you don't want to ruin the trail ride for everybody else, do you?"

"Yes, she does!" Caro said angrily. "She wants everybody to be as miserable as she is! It's not fair!"

Dru began to cry.

It was raining harder now. Emily sighed and stroked Joker's nose. Then she stroked Donna's, so she wouldn't feel left out. It seemed the trail ride she'd been looking forward to wasn't going to happen after all. She tried to tell herself that it wasn't all Dru's fault—it would have rained even if Dru hadn't fallen off her horse. But she couldn't help feeling disappointed—and very mad at Dru!

Pam sighed. "Okay, Fillies, I guess we have to turn back. But don't worry—we'll schedule another

31

overnight trail ride very soon. It's not Dru's fault. Accidents happen sometimes, and the weather report isn't always accurate here in the Adirondacks." She turned back to Dru. "How about getting back up on Donna?" she suggested. "You're not hurt, and it's not a good idea to let a little fall prevent you from riding again. My dad had lots of bad falls when he was riding on the open jumper circuit. But he always got back on again. Come on, Dru. You won't fall off again, I promise."

"I'll walk," Dru said.

Silently, Emily handed her Donna's reins. Emily, Libby, Lynda, and Pam got back on their horses. As the rain misted gently down, Pam led the Fillies back along the trail they had just covered. Dru slogged steadily and stubbornly along, clutching Donna's reins.

It was almost five o'clock when the Fillies finally came in sight of the Webster farm. The minute they reached the stables, Dru dropped Donna's reins and headed for the bunkhouse. She hadn't said a single word during the entire trip. Penny took Donna into her stall and began unsaddling the little mare and rubbing her down. The rest of the girls tended to their own horses, and Pam, after she'd taken care of Firefly, sprinted for the farmhouse to tell her parents what had happened.

Emily was giving Joker a good rubdown when

Chris Webster came by and stuck his head into Joker's stall.

"That Dru is something else," he said, folding his arms on top of the stall door. "I don't think she was hurt at all. She's really weird."

"Weird isn't the word for it!" Caro said from the stall next to Joker's where she was unsaddling Vic. "I will *never* forgive her for this, absolutely never! If you had any idea how long it took me to pack my blanket roll . . . !"

Emily didn't say anything. For once, she knew exactly how Caro felt, and she agreed completely. Still, she felt she ought to at least try to say something positive. The best she could come up with was, "Well, it's raining anyway. We probably would have had to turn back even if Dru hadn't fallen."

As if to emphasize her words, thunder rumbled ominously, and the patter of rain on the stable roof became faster and louder. Joker shifted restlessly and tossed his head. Emily stroked him, murmuring, "Take it easy, boy. Nothing to be afraid of."

"Horses don't like thunder much," Chris said. He glanced over at Vic. "Take Vic now—he really *hates* it."

"*Ouch!*" Caro yelled at the same time. "This rotten horse just stepped on my foot! I'm getting out of here before he kills me!" Quickly she slipped out of the stall, latching it behind her. "If my foot turns black and blue and I get gangrene, my father will sue your father," she told Chris. "I'm going up to

33

the house and have Marie take a look at it. I think that stupid horse broke some of my toes!"

Caro strode off in the direction of the stable door, then paused, scowling at the rain which was coming down in sheets. "Oh, rats! What a perfectly awful, *terrible* day!" She dashed out into the rain, squealing as she ran.

"Her toes aren't broken," Chris said calmly to Emily as he let himself into Vic's stall to give the nervous bay a series of soothing pats. "If they were, she couldn't run like that. I guess Mom's gonna be pretty busy with Dru and Caro. But she'll calm them down. She's good at that."

"I'll bet she is," Emily said. "I guess she has to be with so many campers to look after, as well as all of you."

Chris grinned at her over the partition between Joker's stall and Vic's. "You think it's tough taking care of Warren, Pam, and me?"

"I didn't mean that exactly. At home, there's only my older brother Eric and me—and we live in a town, not on a farm—but sometimes we drive my mom and dad crazy, so I guess you must drive your parents crazy, too . . . sometimes . . . ." That didn't come out quite right. "What I mean is . . . "

"I know what you mean. Yeah, I guess we drive our folks up the wall sometimes. They're not too crazy about Warren's rock group, the River Rats."

"I heard them play last week at the American Legion Hall in Winnepac," Emily said. "I went with the Thoros."

"How'd you like them?" Chris asked.

"Oh, they were really . . . " Emily tried to think of the right word. " . . . loud," she finished lamely.

Chris laughed. "They're loud, all right! I'm not into hard rock music much, but I think they're pretty good. You didn't like them, huh?"

"I didn't say that. I'm not much into hard rock, either, but the rest of the girls thought they were terrific," Emily said. Actually, the music had given her a terrible headache, and she'd been very glad when the performance was over, but she didn't want to tell Chris that. She was enjoying their conversation, and she didn't want him to think she was a dope.

"Every summer, a lot of girls get crushes on Warren," Chris stated cheerfully. "He kind of likes it, but he's going steady with Melinda, the Foals' counselor. Do *you* have a crush on Warren?"

"Me?" Emily's eyes widened. "Oh, for heaven's sake! No." Caro did, she knew—or at least Caro was trying her best to make handsome, seventeen-year-old Warren notice her—but Emily thought that was silly. Emily herself was much more interested in horses than in boys, particularly boys who were four years older than she was. Sometimes she and Judy talked about what it would be like to have a boyfriend, but they'd agreed that they had plenty of time for that.

35

Emily usually didn't know what to say to boys anyway, except her fifteen-year-old brother, Eric—and brothers didn't exactly count. But somehow it was easy to talk to Chris Webster. Maybe it was because he was a horse person, too. She could tell he really loved horses from the way he was taking care of Vic and soothing him so the horse wouldn't be scared of the thunder.

"Okay, fella, you're going to be fine," Chris said, slapping Vic fondly on the flank and letting himself out of the stall. "You coming?" he asked Emily. "If you rub Joker down any more, you're going to rub off all his hair."

Emily giggled. "I certainly wouldn't want to do that!" She kissed Joker's nose and scratched behind his ears, then checked to see that he had plenty of fresh, sweet hay to munch on. Satisfied that he did, she left his stall and carefully latched the door behind her.

"We're not going to let them out into the pasture the way we usually do, are we?" she asked, following Chris to the stable entrance. It was still pouring, though the sky seemed to be a little lighter.

"Not till the rain lets up," Chris said, looking up at the clouds. "It wouldn't hurt them to get wet, though. And I bet it's going to clear up in about . . ." He thought for a moment. " . . . half an hour."

"How do you know that?" Emily asked.

"See those clouds up there?"

She nodded.

"Well, they're starting to break up. And there's a west wind that will blow the storm over the mountains into the next county. It'll take about half an hour, like I said. When you've lived in the Adirondacks all your life, you know about stuff like that."

Emily was impressed. "It must be neat living here all year round," she said. "I bet it's beautiful in winter, when it snows."

"It's beautiful, all right. But sometimes it snows so hard and the drifts are so deep that we can't get down to the main road." Chris grinned. "That's what I like best! Then I can't get to school, even if it's open, which it usually isn't when there's a really *big* snow."

"Don't you like school?" Emily asked.

"It's okay, I guess. But I'd rather be riding."

Emily smiled. "Me, too!"

The rain was slackening now, and Chris said, "I think we better make a run for it. Ready?"

"Ready!"

Laughing, they ran out into the rain.

Chapter 4

When Emily reached the Fillies' bunkhouse, she was soaked. The rest of her cabin mates were still in the process of changing out of their wet clothes and toweling down, but nobody was saying much. About the only sound Emily could hear was Caro's mega-watt electric hair dryer humming away as Caro blow-dried her silvery-blond hair.

"Where've you been, Emily?" Libby called from her upper bunk, where she was struggling into a pair of dry jeans. "What took you so long?"

"I wanted to make sure Joker was good and dry," Emily said, plopping down on the floor and pulling off her boots. As she took off each one, she held it upside down to let the water drain out. Then she peeled off her socks. "Yuck!" she groaned. "My toes are all pruny!"

"Join the club," Lynda said cheerfully. "Prunes Anonymous!"

"Caro, aren't you through with that hair dryer yet?" Danny complained. "You know we can't plug in another one until you're done or we'll blow a fuse, and my hair is positively sopping."

"I'll be finished in a minute," Caro said. "First come, first served, and I was here first."

"As usual," Libby muttered.

Emily began to shuck off her wet jeans. They were cold and clammy—she actually had goose bumps. Even her underwear was soaked. She'd have to change everything from the skin out.

As she rummaged in her trunk for fresh, dry clothes, she glanced over at Dru's bunk. Dru was lying there, face down, covered by a blanket. Emily went over to the upper bunk where Penny was brushing her hair—unbraided for once—and carefully counting every stroke.

"How is she?" Emily whispered.

Penny sighed. "I don't know . . . . seventy-five, seventy-six, seventy-seven. Marie came down to check her out . . . eighty, eighty-one, eighty-two . . . and she said she was okay. She gave Dru some aspirin and told her she didn't have to come up to the house for supper if she didn't want to . . . . ninety-four, ninety-five, ninety-six . . . I think she's sleeping . . . . ninety-nine, one hundred." She put down the hairbrush and began braiding her blond hair again. "But I'm kind of worried about her, to tell the truth. She's still very upset."

Emily looked down at Dru, wondering if there was anything she could do to make her feel better. She couldn't think of a single thing, and besides, she was beginning to shiver from the cool breezes that blew through the cabin. So she shrugged helplessly and took her dry clothes into the bathroom where she could change in privacy. Once inside, she decided to see if there was any hot water left for a quick shower, and found that there was. So she showered, which warmed her up considerably, rubbed herself down as briskly as she had rubbed down Joker, and dressed.

By the time she came out, weak sunlight was filtering through the windows and the rest of the Fillies were getting ready to go up to the house for supper. As Emily was slipping her feet into her socks and sneakers, Pam came into the cabin.

"Hey, Fillies, guess what? Since it's stopped raining, we're going to cook out just the way we would have done on the trail ride, down by the river where we usually have the campfire!" she said. "There's a pavilion there, which you may not have noticed, and it has a big fireplace. Chris is starting the fire now. Come on! You can all help to make the hamburgers and throw them on the grill."

"Big deal," Caro muttered, but the rest of the girls were enthusiastic—except Dru, of course.

40

"Should we leave Dru here all by herself?" Penny asked.

"She'll be all right. All she needs is rest," Pam assured her. "We'll bring her back a hamburger in case she's hungry."

"*In case!*" Caro echoed sarcastically. "When has Dru ever not been hungry?"

"With relish and ketchup, on a toasted bun," Dru muttered into her pillow. "Medium rare."

"See? What did I tell you?"

Caro flounced out after Pam, and the other Fillies followed.

It was true—Emily hadn't noticed the pavilion under the trees down by the river, even though there had been a campfire in the clearing almost every night since she'd been at Webster's. The pavilion was actually just a long, peaked roof supported by roughhewn logs, with a big stone fireplace at one end. Four weathered picnic tables and benches were the only items of furniture. The building was almost completely concealed from the clearing by the trees, but between the tree trunks you could look out across the river to the opposite bank and the mountains beyond.

The grass was wet, the ground outside was squishy, and water dripped from the trees, but inside the pavilion it was pretty dry. When the Fillies arrived, flames were crackling merrily in the fireplace, and Chris was feeding another log into the

41

blaze. The food that had been intended for the Fillies' cookout—hamburgers, buns, ketchup, relish, a big bowl of salad, and a tin that Emily hoped contained lots of Marie's fantastic butterscotch brownies—was heaped on the nearest table next to an insulated bag filled with cans of ice-cold soda.

"Boy, am I ever hungry and thirsty," Danny said, grabbing a soda can. Then she looked at the label and frowned. "What is this stuff? *Sar-sa-pa-rilla?*"

Libby giggled. "That's the way it's spelled, but that's not the way you pronounce it. It's 'sassparilla,' and it tastes kind of like root beer, only better." She took a can, too. "Want one, Emily?"

"No, thanks. I think I'll have birch beer," Emily said. She popped the top on the can and took a long, deep swig. It tasted delicious.

"Isn't there any diet soda?" Caro asked, rummaging through the cans. "I don't know about the rest of you, but I have to watch my figure."

"If you don't, nobody else will, that's for sure," Libby teased, and Emily's giggle almost made her choke on her soda.

"*Some* people don't have any figure to *watch,*" Caro said, eyeing Libby's petite, boyish frame.

"Now cut that out, girls!" Pam ordered. "Do I have any volunteers for burger detail? As soon as the flames die down, we can start grilling."

Lynda and Penny agreed to make the patties, and Danny began distributing paper plates and napkins

42

on one of the other tables, while Libby opened a package of buns and plopped one on each plate.

"I'm going to see if I can find some wildflowers for the table," Caro said. "This place could use some interior decoration." She strolled off, clutching her can of diet orange soda.

"Guess her toes aren't broken after all," Chris said to Emily as he stood up and brushed off his hands on his jeans.

"Guess not," Emily said, grinning. "She didn't say a word about them back at the cabin, and I didn't ask her. If I had, she probably wouldn't have answered. Caro's still not speaking to me."

"Consider yourself lucky!" Chris said. "Seems to me when she does speak, she always says something mean."

"What happened to Caro's toes?" Pam asked as she took the butterscotch brownies from the tin and piled them on a paper plate. "Something I should know about?"

"Nope," Chris replied. "Vic got spooked by the thunder, the way he does, and he started dancing around while Caro was rubbing him down. She said he stepped on her foot and if she got gangrene, her dad would sue our dad. You know the way she talks. She said she was going to go and have Mom look at her toes, but I don't think she did."

Pam sighed. "Really! Between Caro and Dru, sometimes I just don't know which end is up! This isn't exactly the easiest bunch of Fillies we've ever

43

had." Then she glanced at Emily, and added, "Sorry, Emily. I don't mean you, or any of the other girls, either."

"That's okay. I know how you feel," Emily said. "Only, I can't help worrying about Dru. I think that she fell off Donna on purpose because she didn't want to go on the trail ride. I mean, you'd really have to work at it to fall off that horse!"

"Better believe it," Pam agreed. "Mom and Dad have been running this camp for seven years, and we've had Donna for five, and no one's ever fallen off her before, not even a Foal!"

"Hey, Pam, it looks like the fire's ready to start grilling," Lynda said. "Can we put the burgers on?"

Pam went over to the fireplace and poked at the burning logs with a stick. "Sure. You want to be the cook, Lynda?"

"Why not?" Lynda said. "C'mon, Penny, want to give me a hand?"

"Okay." Penny picked up a paper plate piled high with hamburger patties—and tripped over a tree root that was sticking up out of the ground. The hamburgers went flying, landing on the dirt floor covered with pine needles.

"Oh, no!" she cried. "I'm so sorry! I never did anything like this at Girl Scout camp!"

Danny and Libby ran over and joined Penny, Lynda, Emily, and Pam as they started picking up the patties.

"Don't worry about it, Penny," Pam said cheer-

fully. "No harm done. We'll just dust 'em off and grill 'em anyway. It's not like they fell into a pigpen or anything. The only person who might possibly mind is Caro—"

"And she's not here!" Chris chimed in, grinning.

"I have a great idea!" Libby chortled. "How about we make a Caro Special—stick a bunch of pine needles in the middle of her burger? We could tell her it's a fancy gourmet treat!"

"Cool it, Libby," Pam said, trying to frown. But the idea obviously appealed to her. "Come on, Fillies—and Chris. Let's start cleaning up these burgers."

It didn't take long before every single needle had been carefully removed and the patties had been placed on the iron grill over the embers. Soon the scent of broiling meat mingled with the smell of hickory smoke and pine. Emily's stomach was growling so loudly she was sure everybody could hear it. But when she apologized for the sound, Libby said, *"Your* stomach? I thought it was mine!"

"Or mine," Danny said.

"Mine, too!" Chris added. "Boy, am I starved!"

"That smells absolutely divine," Caro cried as she came into the pavilion clutching a bunch of limp wildflowers in her hand. "Make mine *very* rare, please . . . on second thought, I'm so hungry I think I'd better have two. But no buns. No, make that *one* bun, lightly toasted. I'll put one burger on each half. Not as many carbohydrates that way. Pam, do we

46

have a vase or something I could put these flowers in? No? Oh, well, I guess you can't have *everything*."

Emily couldn't remember eating anything in her entire life that tasted better than those burgers. Penny had trotted off to the Fillies' cabin with a medium-rare burger with relish and ketchup on a toasted bun for Dru, and reported when she returned that Dru had sat up in her bunk and had eaten the whole thing, as well as the salad Penny had brought and two butterscotch brownies, washed down by a can of cola.

"Dru's feeling much better," Penny told everybody. "I think she's going to be just fine in the morning. I don't think she noticed the—" Penny stopped dead, pressing her fingers to her mouth.

"Noticed what?" Caro asked innocently.

"Nothing! Nothing! Dru enjoyed her meal, and that's the important thing," Pam said quickly. "Hey, Fillies, let's throw all the paper plates and napkins and stuff into the fire, and then we can take a walk down by the river and watch the sunset. It ought to be really beautiful after that storm. Then maybe we'll sing for a while. Chris, did you bring your guitar?"

Emily was surprised to hear that Chris played the guitar. Warren had played at campfires from time to time, but not his younger brother.

"Yeah, I brought it," Chris said, tossing crumpled paper plates and napkins into the flames. "I'll play if you really want me to. But I'm not as good as Warren, you know."

Pam smiled at him. "I like the way you play. After our walk, okay?"

"Okay," Chris mumbled.

"Why can't Warren come down and play for us?" Caro wanted to know. "He's a *real* musician."

"Warren has practice with the River Rats tonight. He's probably already left for Winnepac," Pam said. "So has Melinda. She's the Rats' lead singer, you know."

Caro rolled her eyes. "How could I possibly forget?"

The Fillies tramped through the damp grass down to the bank of the river. The sky was turning all shades of pink, purple, and gold, and the colors were reflected in the waters of the Winnepac. One sailboat skimmed over the surface of the river like a waterbird, its multicolored sails catching the last of the evening sun. Night birds were beginning to call their plaintive cries from the trees on the banks, and the smell of pine was everywhere.

Emily wished—oh, how she wished!—that Judy could be with her. The thought of her very best friend in all the world sitting with her leg in a cast back home dimmed the radiance of this glorious evening. Emily would write to Judy about it, but it wouldn't be the same. She wished she was a good enough writer to describe to Judy how beautiful it was, but she knew she wasn't.

"What's the matter, Emily? You look kind of sad," Libby said, trotting up next to her.

Emily smiled wistfully. "I was just thinking about how much Judy would have enjoyed this," she admitted. Libby knew about Judy and her broken leg.

"Well, she'll be here next summer, won't she?" Libby asked. "This isn't the only sunset we'll ever see. It happens all the time, and I don't imagine it'll stop happening next year!"

Emily's smile broadened. "You have a point there," she said. "I'll definitely be coming back, and Judy will be coming with me. You will, too, won't you, Libby?"

"I sure will! I'll be coming to Webster's until I'm a famous jockey—and even then, I'll probably drop in to say hello every now and then."

"What happened to Penny?" Danny asked as she joined Emily and Libby. "She kind of disappeared. Think I ought to tell Pam?"

"No," Emily said. "She probably went to the bunkhouse to check on Dru. She'll be back in a minute."

The girls continued to wander along the riverbank, paying no attention to their sneakers, which were becoming wetter by the minute because of the damp grass. The sunset got more and more brilliant, then began to fade into soft mauve and rose as a crisp crescent moon became sharp and clear over the mountains. Pam pointed out an island in the river where deer came at twilight to feed. Two

49

people in a canoe glided silently past, silhouetted against the fading light.

"She's gone!"

Penny's strident voice broke into the Fillies' reverie.

"Dru's gone! I went back to see how she was, and she wasn't there!" Penny ran over to Pam and clutched her arm. "She ate everything I brought her, and then she *left*! I went up to the farmhouse to ask Matt and Marie if she'd been there, and they said no. They don't know where she is, and I don't either. Pam, we have to find her!"

Chapter 5

"Now hold on a minute, Penny," Pam said calmly, putting her arm around the girl's shoulders. "Catch your breath. You're puffing like you've just run the four-minute mile, and that's not good for your digestion."

"But Dru . . . " Penny gasped. "She's *gone*! I'm sure something terrible has happened to her!"

The rest of the Fillies clustered around Penny and Pam, and Chris came over, too.

"Maybe she just decided to go for a walk," Emily suggested. "She must have been feeling a lot better after her supper, and she probably looked out the window and saw how beautiful the sunset was, so she took a walk."

"Yeah, Penny," Libby said, "I bet that's it. I bet she went down to where we swim to look at the sunset."

"Or maybe she felt so much better, she decided to come up here and join us," Danny added. "She knew we had the makings for s'mores, and she wouldn't want to miss that. Dru loves s'mores. You probably just missed her. She might be coming up one of the other paths this very minute."

"She might have gone to the sheep pasture to see the lambs, like you asked her to yesterday," Lynda said. "I don't think there's anything to worry about, Penny."

"*I* don't see what all the fuss is about." Caro folded her arms across her chest. "She's bound to turn up any second now."

But Penny wasn't convinced. She shook her head stubbornly, making her neat blond braids swing back and forth. "You don't know Dru like I do," she said. "Dru's not the type to go off by herself and look at the sunset, or the lambs, or anything. Dru is . . . well, she's . . . "

"*Weird!*" Caro said.

"Lonely," Penny corrected angrily. She looked up at Pam. "I really think we ought to look for her. She was really miserable today. There's no telling what she might do!"

Pam hugged Penny, then looked down at her unhappy little face. "Penny, I know you're worried about your friend because you care about her. Dru's lucky to have a friend like you. But now tell me—did you look around the camp, go down to the dock, check out the sheep pasture, stuff like that?"

Penny shook her head again, less violently this time. "I—I didn't think . . . "

"Did you check the rec room at the house, where the TV is, and the VCR? Dru might have decided to watch TV, or a tape of a movie."

"Like *National Velvet,*" Danny said eagerly.

"No . . . but Matt and Marie said she wasn't at the house."

"Hey, Mom and Dad might not have known she was there," Chris said. "The Foals were putting on skits, and the Thoros were going to some square dance at Long Branch tonight. Mom was helping with the Foals, and Dad was going to drive the Thoros over the bridge to Long Branch in the van."

"A square dance? At Long Branch?" Caro was suddenly interested. Long Branch was the boys' camp directly across the Winnepac River. "That was *tonight*? I thought it was next week. I wanted to go, too!"

"Well, you missed it," Libby said, smiling impishly. "Too bad, Caro."

"Rachel was supposed to be in charge tonight," Pam said. "Did you talk to Rachel, Penny? She might have known where Dru was."

"No . . . I didn't see Rachel at all," Penny admitted. She twisted one braid in her hand and bit her lip. "I guess I didn't think about much of anything except that Dru wasn't where she was supposed to be."

"That's okay," Pam said gently. "When you're

upset, you can't think of everything." She gave Penny a little pat, then released her. "But anyway, I think it would be a good idea to pack up all our stuff and go back to the cabin. If Dru isn't there, we'll send out a search party. But I bet she will be!"

"I guess if she was coming up another trail to join us, she'd have been here by now," Danny said, "so I guess she isn't coming. Too bad about the s'mores . . . ."

"Come on, gang, let's get with it," Pam sang out. But Emily could tell that she wasn't as cheerful as she pretended to be. As she headed back to the pavilion with the other Fillies, Emily wondered where Dru was. It was getting dark—the sunset glow had faded, and the crescent moon was brighter now in a purplish sky. Night birds were calling from the treetops, and the evening star shone clearly above the tallest pine. Everything was still beautiful, but different somehow.

Beneath the roof of the pavilion, it was even darker. The dying embers provided the only light as the Fillies, Pam, and Chris packed up what was left of their picnic. Chris ran down to the river and brought back water to douse the fire. Everyone picked up a bag and followed Pam at a brisk pace across the clearing, back to the comfortable, welcoming lights of the farmhouse and the cabins. Nobody had much to say.

"Bat!" Caro suddenly screamed, flailing her arms around wildly as a dark shape flitted through the

54

trees. "That was a *bat*! Bats get tangled in your hair and then they suck your blood! And after I spent so much time with the blow dryer!"

"*Our* bats don't suck your blood," Chris's voice rang out next to Emily. "And they don't mess around with people's hair, either. I bet you believe in Dracula, too, don't you?"

"Oh, what do *you* know!" But Caro started walking a lot faster than she had been.

"You're supposed to wear garlic around your neck, and make the sign of the cross over your windows if there's a vampire around," Danny whispered to Emily as they hurried toward the camp. "Not that I believe in vampires or anything, but you never can tell."

Emily wasn't concerned about vampire bats. But she was very concerned about Dru. She tried to tell herself that Dru would be sitting on her bunk, or maybe fast asleep, when they came in. And yet somehow she couldn't believe it.

"She's not here."

Penny was the first to enter the Fillies' bunkhouse, and when she switched on the overhead light, it was apparent that the cabin was completely empty.

"There's her paper plate," Lynda said, running over to Dru's bunk and picking up the soggy plate.

"I *told* you she ate her burger!" Penny cried. "That doesn't prove anything."

"I'm going to bed," Caro said. "When you find Dru sitting in front of the TV, please try to keep it down to a slight roar. I really don't want to know about it." She began stripping out of her clothes.

"I'll go up to the house and check right now," Pam said. "I bet that's just where she is. It's much too dark for her to be wandering around outside."

"Can I come with you?" Penny asked anxiously.

"Why not?" Pam agreed.

"Me, too?" Emily asked. She decided she couldn't possibly sleep until she knew that Dru was all right.

"Sure. The more, the merrier." But again, the hearty sound of Pam's voice didn't reflect the concern Emily saw on her face. "The rest of you guys get ready for bed. It's been a long day."

Emily and Penny trotted beside Pam as she headed for the farmhouse. The sky was deep purple now, and the evening star had been joined by many others overhead. The little crescent moon smiled down on them as though nothing could possibly be wrong. Crickets chirped cheerfully all around.

"What if she's not there, Pam?" Penny murmured. "What do we do then?"

"We'll cross that bridge when we come to it," Pam said.

Dru wasn't in the living room, but Warren was. "I thought you had practice tonight," Pam said. "Canceled," Warren mumbled without taking his

56

eyes off the TV screen where a tape of an adventure movie was playing.

"Have you seen Dru?" Pam asked.

"The fat little girl with braces?" Pam nodded, and Warren shook his head. "Nope. Last I saw of her was when you guys were taking off on your overnight trail ride. What's the matter, did you lose her or something?"

"I didn't *lose* her!" Pam snapped. "She's just missing, that's all."

"You lost her," Warren said, keeping his gaze on the television screen. "What're you going to do about it?"

"Warren, turn that thing *off*!"

Emily had never heard Pam yell like that, and apparently neither had Warren. He pressed a button on the remote control, and the picture froze.

"So what do you want *me* to do about it?" Warren asked.

Pam ran her fingers through her hair. "I want you to help us look for her!"

Warren stood up. "Hey, cool out, Pam. How far could she have gone? She's only—what?—twelve or something. How far could a twelve-year-old go?"

"I don't *know*!" Pam paced back and forth across the big, pine-paneled room. "All I know is, she's not in the Fillies' cabin, and she didn't show up at the pavilion, and nobody knows where she is, and it's *dark* out there! We have to find her, Warren, and you have to help us."

"Dru was very unhappy today," Penny said softly. "She didn't want to go on the trail ride, and when she did, she fell off Donna—"

"She fell off *Donna*?" Warren looked astonished. "Come on! *Nobody* falls off Donna!"

"Well, Dru did," Emily said. "That's one of the reasons we came back. The rain was the other reason, but Dru wanted to come back, rain or no rain. She walked all the way."

"And then Marie—your mother—told Dru to rest, so she did, and I brought her a hamburger, and she ate it, and then when I came back to check on her, Dru wasn't in her bunk," Penny said, all in a rush. "And she still isn't, and so we have to find her and bring her back!"

"Wow!" Warren said. "We've never lost a Filly before. Or a Foal or a Thoro, either. Guess we better find her."

"I think that's what I said about an hour ago," Pam said grimly. "I don't want to worry Mom, and Dad's not back yet from Long Branch, so it's up to us."

"What's up to you?"

Marie came into the room just then. In her plaid shirt and faded jeans, she didn't look much older than the counselors, but Emily knew that Marie was about the same age as her own mother.

"What's going on?" Marie asked.

"We've lost a Filly," Warren said. "The fat one with braces."

"Dru? Oh, dear!" Marie's tanned face suddenly looked as worried as the rest of them felt. "What do you mean, we lost her?"

Pam and Warren explained, and Marie's expression became more and more concerned.

"Warren, saddle up Zep, and ride along the riverbank. Chris, you take Buster, and scout out the pastures and comb the woods. Pam, take Emily and Penny back to the Fillies' bunkhouse, and tell the rest of the girls that we're looking for Dru—try not to alarm them too much." She glanced at Penny and Emily and smiled reassuringly. "I'm sure she's perfectly all right. From what little I know of Dru, I suspect that she might have decided to run away . . . . " Her smile faded. "I knew she wasn't happy here, and I tried to get her to talk about it, but she didn't seem to want to. I should have tried harder."

"Dru doesn't talk much," Penny said, "not even to me, and I'm her best friend at Webster's."

"It's not your fault, Mom," Pam added. "After I tell the Fillies what's happening, I'll take Firefly and help Chris and Warren search."

"Good idea," Marie said. "Oh, dear, I wish your father was here, but he's not due back with the Thoros for another hour or so. Anyway, I'll drive the pickup down the road to Winnepac. Dru might have headed for town. Okay, gang, let's get moving. And if—*when* one of us finds her, bring her straight back here. In any event, I want everybody to meet here in an hour and a half to compare notes."

Emily couldn't help thinking that even though Pam looked a lot like her father, she acted and sounded very much like her mother when she was dealing with a crisis. Emily was comforted by Marie's take-charge attitude.

Warren picked up his denim jacket from the couch, slung it over his shoulder, and strode out of the room with Chris right behind him.

"Marie . . . " Penny faltered.

"What is it, honey?"

"Well, I'm Dru's best friend, and I'm really worried about her. Could I . . . would you let me . . . I mean, can I . . . "

Marie seemed to read Penny's mind. "Want to come with me in the pickup?"

Penny nodded eagerly.

"Sure. Come on, let's go!" She took Penny's hand, and the two of them hurried off.

Emily looked after them wistfully. She wished she'd thought to ask if she could go, too, but it was too late now.

"Emily? You coming?" Pam asked, and Emily nodded.

As they walked toward the Fillies' bunkhouse, Emily noticed how pitch black it was outside. Wherever Dru was, she had to be scared out of her mind, all alone in the night. Emily knew *she* would have been scared, with bats flying around and owls hooting, and everything looking strange and menacing. Judy wouldn't, though. If Judy were here and had

61

decided to run away, she would have thought it was an exciting adventure. But Judy *wouldn't* have run away, unless it was just for fun, and Emily knew that fun wasn't what Dru had in mind. What *did* Dru have in mind? Emily simply didn't know.

Chapter 6

"What's happening?"

"Did you find Dru?"

"What did Marie say?"

Libby, Lynda, and Danny peppered Pam and Emily with questions the minute they walked in the door. Caro was curled up in her bunk, her face to the wall.

"Cool it, Fillies," Pam said calmly. "What's happening is that Warren and Chris are looking around the camp, and Mom's taking the pickup down the road to Winnepac to look for Dru. I'm going to help Chris and Warren search, too, as soon as I leave here. Don't worry—she can't have gone very far. I'm positive we'll find her very soon, and that she's perfectly okay."

"Where's Penny?" Lynda asked.

"She's going with Mom in the truck."

Sitting up cross-legged in her bunk, Danny said, "Maybe Dru's been *kidnapped*! I read this book once about a gang of criminals who kidnapped a girl, and they held her for ransom for *weeks*! They said if the parents didn't pay up, they'd start sending locks of her *hair*!" Danny shuddered.

"Did they pay up?" Libby asked.

"Yes, but only after they'd gotten an envelope in the mail absolutely *filled* with her hair! The kidnappers got caught, though, so it had a happy ending."

"Wow!" Linda exclaimed.

"That's ridiculous!" Caro rolled over and sat up, brushing wisps of her own silvery-blond hair out of her eyes. "People don't kidnap other people unless they know somebody has lots of money to pay the ransom. If anybody was going to be kidnapped, it would have been *me*. My folks would pay a *fortune* to get me back."

"I wonder why," Libby murmured.

"I am absolutely sure that Dru hasn't been kidnapped," Pam said, glaring at Caro. "We all know that Dru wasn't having a very good time here at camp, and I'm also sure that we're all sorry about that. Mom thinks she might have run away. If she has, it's really important that when we find her we show her we like her a lot, and try to make her feel at home here . . . the way most of you feel."

"That depends on what you mean by 'home'," Caro said. "This isn't anything like what *I'm* used to at home!"

64

"Hey, Caro, go back to sleep, will you?" Lynda snapped.

"Give me a break, okay?" Pam said, becoming annoyed by the arguing. "You're all grown up enough not to need a baby-sitter, so I'm taking off. I'll check in later and let you all know when we find Dru. And we *will* find her! Mom, Chris, Warren, and I are going to search every inch of the property."

"Warren?" Caro's big, beautiful eyes widened. "Warren's looking for Dru, too?"

"Of course he is," Pam said impatiently. "And I'm on my way to help him. See you."

She strode out of the cabin, and Caro wrapped her arms around her knees. "Warren's looking for Dru! Gee, now I really wish somebody had kidnapped *me*! I can just see Warren Webster breaking into their hideout and rescuing me!"

"Even if you were missing most of your hair?" Danny asked. "Even if you were *bald*?"

"It just might be worth it," Caro mused aloud. "Warren is so gorgeous.. . . . "

"Go to sleep, Caro," Libby said. "Or at least shut up, okay? You're giving me a royal pain."

"Some people have no imagination." Caro pounded her pillow and rolled over onto her stomach. "Will somebody please turn out the light? I can't sleep when there's a light in my eyes."

Emily reached over and flicked the switch—not because Caro had requested it, but because there didn't seem to be anything else she could do. She wandered over to her bunk and sat down on the edge of it, clasping her hands in her lap. Her mind was filled with pictures: Dru playing Monopoly with Penny on the floor of the cabin; Dru hanging on to Donna's saddle for dear life; Dru lying on the ground, scared and hurt. And then she thought of Dru trudging silently back down the trail to Webster's in the rain, clutching Donna's reins. Dru was a sad person. Emily didn't really understand sad people—she'd never run into one before, at least not one who was almost her own age. What had made Dru so sad? Didn't any of the rest of the Fillies care? Penny cared, and Marie did, too. Now Marie and Penny were driving through the night, trying to find Dru.

"Aren't you going to go to bed, Emily?" Libby whispered from the upper bunk. "I'm just about asleep."

"In a minute," Emily replied. All she had to do was put on her pajamas and crawl into her bunk like everyone else. Pam had said she'd let them know when they found Dru.

But what if they *didn't* find Dru? What if Dru was in real danger? What if she'd fallen into the river or something? What if . . . ?

Emily waited until the sound of quiet breathing told her that Libby, Lynda, Danny, and Caro were fast asleep. Then she slipped off her sneakers and shoved her feet into her riding boots. She looked at the digital clock on the bureau. It was nine-thirty—only forty-five minutes until everybody was supposed to return to the farmhouse to make their reports.

Walking on tiptoe, Emily moved to the door. When she had closed it behind her, she breathed a sigh of relief. What she intended to do was against all the rules, but she had to do it. She couldn't just lie there in her bunk, worrying. She was going to help look for Dru, even though the Websters would probably be mad at her for taking Joker out without permission and without supervision. What kind of punishment would they give her? Emily wondered apprehensively. Maybe she wouldn't be allowed to ride in the horse show on Sunday. Or maybe they wouldn't let her ride at all next week. Or, worst of all, what if Matt decided to assign Joker to Caro and give Emily some other horse? That thought was so awful that Emily almost turned back.

But she didn't. She'd rather be punished than know that she might have helped find Dru and hadn't even tried. If she didn't at least try, she'd never stop feeling guilty about how angry she'd been at Dru for ruining the trail ride. Maybe if she'd been nicer to Dru, Emily thought, Dru would have known she had another friend besides Penny, and maybe she wouldn't have run away.

Emily began to run, cutting across the wet grass rather than following the path to the stable. She was glad to see that the lights were on—she wasn't exactly sure where the switch was, and she hadn't been looking forward to saddling Joker in the dark.

As she entered the stable, most of the horses stuck their heads out over their stall doors and looked curiously at her.

"Hi, fellas," Emily said softly as she walked along, patting each nose she passed. "Guess you're not used to so many people coming and going late at night, are you? You're usually not even here at night, but because of the rain and all the excitement, nobody remembered to let you out into the pasture."

At the sound of her voice, Joker whickered a greeting. Emily let herself into his stall, then put her arms around his neck and gave him a big hug.

"Dru's missing," she told him. "That's why Pam and Chris and Warren took their horses out tonight—they're searching for her. And we're going to search, too! I'll probably get in trouble, but I'm going to do it anyway." She pressed her cheek against him. "Maybe they won't let me ride you after tonight, and if that happens, I'll hate it something fierce. But I just want you to know that even if you won't be my horse anymore, I'll keep on loving you just as much."

Joker snorted and nodded his golden head. Emily was sure he understood everything she said. That was why she talked to him all the time. Caro thought she was crazy talking to a horse, but Emily really didn't care what Caro thought.

She left the stall to get Joker's saddle, bridle, and saddle pad down from the rack where she had placed them earlier that day. She slipped off his halter and put on the bridle, then quickly saddled him, double-checking to make sure the girth was tight enough. Satisfied that she'd done everything right, Emily led him out of the stable to the mounting block and swung up onto his back.

"Okay, boy, here we go!" she whispered, then hesitated. *Where* were they going? Down to the river? No, Warren was patroling the riverbank, and Emily figured he wouldn't welcome her help. Pam and Chris were supposed to be covering the pastures and the woods. That was much bigger territory—they couldn't possibly cover every inch of it. Emily decided to head for the woods. It would be very easy for someone like Dru to get lost among all those trees.

Someone like Dru. If I was a shy person who was easily frightened, would I go into the woods where it's dark and scary? Emily asked herself. *Not on your life! I'd be terrified that there might be wild animals out there—maybe even a bear. No, if I were Dru, I think I'd start walking down the road that leads to Winnepac. I bet Marie's right—Dru would have headed for town.*

Emily knew that Marie and Penny were on their way to town in the pickup, but she decided to ride in that direction anyway. It would be easy to miss somebody in the dark, especially somebody who didn't want to be found and who might hide when she saw headlights approaching. Emily clucked to Joker and urged him into a slow trot.

Once they reached the road, she let him trot faster until they had left the farmhouse far behind, then she slowed him to a walk. It was very quiet, except for the chirping of crickets, and very dark. In the velvet black sky, millions of stars twinkled merrily, and the crescent moon shone like a sliver of silver, but little light was shed on the earth below. A light breeze riffled Emily's short, wavy hair—and suddenly she realized that she was *really* in trouble. She'd forgotten to put on her hard hat, and no camper at Webster's was *ever* supposed to ride without one. Well, too late now. If she went back to get it, she might as well never have started out.

"Dru?" Emily called softly. "Dru, it's me, Emily. Dru, are you there?"

No reply, except from the crickets.

"*Dru!*" she called again, louder this time. "Dru, where are you?" She wished she'd thought to bring her flashlight; she could have turned it on the trees and bushes on either side of the road. "No flashlight, no hard hat. Some searcher you are!" she told herself aloud.

Emily reached the pasture where she had seen the beautiful chestnut horse on the first day that she arrived at Webster's. She remembered seeing a ramshackle building there, something like an old, neglected shack. Could Dru have gotten too tired to

walk further and decided to stay in the shack overnight? It was worth a look.

Emily guided Joker up the bank and walked him along the split rail fence until she found a sagging gate. She dismounted, opened the gate, and led Joker through, closing the gate behind her. The grass was very tall and very wet. Emily slogged through it, leading Joker and calling, "Dru? Dru! It's Emily. Dru, if you're there, answer me!"

Nothing but crickets.

When she reached the shack Emily peered inside, and her heart sank. Even in the dark, she could tell it was empty.

She sighed and led Joker back to the gate. After they came out, she climbed up on the fence, using it as a mounting block so she could get back into the saddle.

"Okay, boy, back to the road."

By the time Emily and Joker had reached the point where the road connected with the blacktop to Winnepac, Emily was sure that Dru wasn't anywhere around. She turned Joker back, urging him into a canter. She knew it had to be almost time for Marie and Penny, Chris, Warren, and Pam to meet back at the house, and she hadn't helped at all. She didn't know what else to do. But she kept telling herself that maybe one of them had found Dru, and everything was all right.

"Who's that?"

Emily almost jumped out of her skin at the sound of Chris's voice. She pulled Joker to a walk and said weakly, "It's me, Emily."

"*Emily?* What're you doing out here?"

Chris rode out of the trees on Buster, beaming his flashlight on Emily and Joker. They were not very far from the farmhouse.

"Uh . . . well, I wanted to help find Dru, so I . . . I kind of . . . " Emily couldn't put the words together, but she didn't need to. There she was on Joker, as Chris could plainly see for himself. "Did you find her?" she asked hopefully.

Chris shook his head. "Nope. No sign of her. Last time I saw Pam, she hadn't found her, either." He switched off the flashlight and rode beside Emily down the road. "I didn't see Warren at all. Maybe he or Mom had better luck." They came around a bend in the road, and Emily saw the pickup parked in front of the house. Firefly and Led Zeppelin were tethered to the fence.

"They're here," Chris said. "Tell you what, Emily, you take Joker to the stable and then come back to the house if you want to. I won't say anything about you taking Joker out, okay?"

Emily smiled. "Thanks, Chris! But I'll tell Matt and Marie myself, honest I will, after we see if anybody found Dru. Who knows, she might be sitting in the living room this very minute!"

Chapter 7

Wouldn't it be wonderful, Emily thought as she rode down the path to the stable, if Dru really had been found? It would be so terrific if, when Emily walked into the house, she'd see Dru sitting on the sofa beside Penny, perfectly fine.

Emily swung down out of the saddle and led Joker into the stable.

"Yes, it's us again," she told the interested horses as she hurried to Joker's stall. She was so eager to find out what had happened that she was tempted for a moment to leave his saddle and bridle on—but only for a moment. It wouldn't be right not to take off his tack and give him a quick rubdown, even though he wasn't sweaty at all. It would be as if somebody had forced Emily to get into bed wearing her boots and all her clothes, and she knew she'd hate that.

So she unsaddled Joker as quickly as she could and took off his bridle. He was sweating a little under the saddle pad, she noticed. She dashed out of the stall, lugging his tack, and returned the saddle and bridle to their proper places, then ran to the empty stall opposite the tack room, where brushes, currycombs, rubbing cloths, and other grooming equipment were stored. Emily was in such a hurry, and the light was so dim, that she didn't see the mound of horse blankets on the floor—until she tripped over it.

Emily let out a little squawk as she landed right on top of it.

So did the mound.

Scrambling to her feet, Emily stared wide-eyed down at the blankets. Was one of the stable cats curled up in there?

Suddenly the blankets began to heave and thrash around, making muffled moaning sounds.

A bear! Emily thought, terrified. The stable door had been open all night. Maybe a bear had wandered in, looking for someplace warm and dry to sleep!

She was backing away toward the door when the mound gave one last gigantic lurch, and a round, frightened face emerged.

"Dru!" Emily cried in astonishment. "I thought you were a bear!"

"I thought *you* were a bear, or maybe a mountain lion," Dru said in a quavering voice.

The two girls stared at each other for a split second in total silence, both too shaken to speak. Emily recovered first.

"Where *were* you?" she gasped. "Have you been here all the time? Are you all right? Everybody's been going crazy looking for you!"

Instead of answering, Dru exploded in a series of sneezes. When she finally stopped, she sat up, pushing the blankets away. "Horse hair," she wheezed. "Horse hair, and straw, and dust! My nose is all itchy."

"Here, have a tissue." Emily dug in the pocket of her jeans and pulled one out. "And gesundheit," she added belatedly.

"Thanks." Dru blew her nose loudly several times, then began dusting herself off.

Emily still couldn't quite believe her eyes. Here was Dru, a little dusty and tousled but unharmed, and for nearly two hours six people had been searching high and low for her!

"Dru, aren't you going to *say* anything?" she asked at last.

Dru shrugged silently.

"Penny's been terribly worried about you," Emily said. "We all were. Marie and Pam and Chris and Warren formed a search party, and Penny went with Marie. They're all up at the farmhouse right now. Come on, Dru. Come with me. We have to show them you're okay, or I bet they'll call the police!"

Dru just shook her head.

Now Emily was beginning to get angry. She strode over to where Dru sat and grabbed both her hands, hauling Dru to her feet. "All right, don't talk to me if you don't want to! But you're coming with me, whether you like it or not—you've got to talk to Marie, and to Penny. Don't you care how worried everybody's been? We thought maybe you'd fallen into the river and drowned or something! We thought maybe you were *dead*!"

"Did you really?" Dru brightened a little. "Gee, I didn't think anybody would even notice I was gone."

She pulled one hand out of Emily's grip, but Emily held tightly to the other one, tugging Dru along beside her.

"That is the dumbest thing I ever heard!" Emily fumed. "How could we not notice you were gone? You're not exactly invisible, you know! You could at least have left a note telling us where you were going. Where *were* you going, by the way?"

Dru trotted reluctantly at Emily's side as they left the stable and headed up the path to the farmhouse. "I couldn't tell anyone where I was going because I didn't know where I was going," she panted. "I wasn't going *to* anywhere—I was just going *away* from Webster's!"

"You didn't get very far, did you?" Emily said dryly.

"No, I didn't." Dru gulped and started to cry. "I can't do *anything* right, not even running away!"

Emily fished another tissue out of her pocket and shoved it at Dru. *I feel sorry for her. I do feel sorry for her. I won't get mad at her for feeling so sorry for herself,* she thought over and over. *I will be her friend if it kills me!*

"Listen, Dru," Emily said, slowing her pace a little, "maybe you think you're the only camper at Webster's who's been homesick and unhappy, but that's not true. When I first came here, I was awfully homesick for a while. I missed my family and my best friend, but I got over it because everybody here is so nice. Well, almost everybody," she added, thinking of Caro. "I bet a lot of girls feel that way."

"It's not the same," Dru mumbled, dabbing at her eyes. "You're the kind of person people like. I'm not. Nobody really likes me here, except Penny. And I'm *not* homesick. You can't be homesick unless you have a home. And I don't."

Emily stared at her. "What do you mean, you don't have a home? Sure you do. You have a mother and a father, and two sisters and a brother. You must live somewhere, in a house or an apartment or something."

Dru just shook her head. "You don't understand," she sighed.

No, Emily most definitely didn't. But they had reached the farmhouse now, and Emily tugged at Dru's hand. "Come on, Dru," she urged. "Let's go in. Everybody's going to be so happy to see you!"

"If they are, it's because it would be bad publicity

79

for Webster's if they lost a camper," Dru said. "They won't be happy because they care about me. Maybe Penny will, but that's because she's kind of a misfit, like I am."

"Penny's *not* a misfit," Emily said hotly. "Penny's really nice, and she really likes you."

She flung open the front door and marched inside, still keeping a firm grip on Dru. She ran down the hall and burst into the living room, shoving Dru ahead of her.

"I found her!" Emily cried. "Look, here she is! And she's just fine!"

Marie, Warren, Pam, and Chris stared, open-mouthed. As for Penny, she leaped out of the chair where she had been sitting and raced across the room, throwing her arms around Dru.

"Oh, Dru, I'm so glad!" Penny cried.

"Where was she?"

"Where did you find her?"

"Dru, are you really all right?"

"Where the heck have you been?"

Marie came over and hugged both Penny and Dru, then turned to Emily and hugged her, too. "Thank you, Emily. I don't know how you did it, but I couldn't be happier!"

Emily felt herself blushing. "It was kind of an accident," she said. "At first I thought she was a cat, and then I thought she was a bear . . . . " She realized she wasn't making much sense, but nobody seemed to care.

"Warren, call the state police again and tell them Dru's been found," Marie said, and Warren immediately picked up the phone. Taking Dru's hand, Marie led her to the sofa and sat her down. Penny sat down next to her, beaming happily. Emily sat on the edge of a chair nearby.

As Pam joined Marie, Penny, and Dru, Chris came over to Emily. "Nice work," he whispered. "I didn't tell about you taking Joker out."

"Thanks," Emily said, smiling. "But I'm still going to let them know about it. It wouldn't be right not to."

Chris tapped her lightly on the shoulder, the way her brother Eric did sometimes to let her know he thought she was okay. Then he said to Marie, "Mom, there's no reason for me to stick around anymore, is there? I'll take the horses back to the stable, and then I'm sacking out, okay?"

Marie smiled and nodded. "Absolutely. Thanks, Chris."

He ambled out of the room. But before he left, he turned to Emily and said, "See you."

"Yeah—see you." Emily decided that she liked Chris Webster a lot.

Warren hung up the phone. "I called off the police," he said. "I told Melinda I'd meet her in town. Okay if I take the pickup?"

"Sure. Don't be too late."

Marie leaned against the back of the sofa, putting one arm around Dru. "Dru, honey, I can't possibly

81

tell you how glad we all are to have you back. We were worried out of our minds. Want to tell us about it?"

"About what?" Dru muttered, looking down at her lap.

"Everything!" Penny cried. "Where you went, and why you went, and . . . well, everything. I was so scared when I went back to the cabin to see how you were feeling and you weren't there!"

"Yes, Dru, we were all scared," Pam said, sitting on the arm of the sofa next to Marie.

"I bet Caro wasn't scared. She probably thought 'good riddance to bad rubbish.' "

"That's just the way Caro is," Emily put in. "I think she was jealous because the rest of us were so worried about you."

"Were you really? *Really* worried about me?" Dru asked, raising her head and looking around at everyone.

"Yes, Dru, we really were," Marie said, pulling Dru close. "At Webster's, we think of our campers as part of our family for the summer. That's why we like to keep our enrollment small. Otherwise, we'd lose track of our girls. And Dru, I feel really bad because I think that somehow I lost track of you. I should have known how unhappy you were, and I should have done something about it."

"That's okay," Dru said softly. "I'm the kind of person people lose track of. It's not your fault."

"Hey, Dru, I bet you're hungry, right?" Pam said,

standing up. "How about a little snack? I think we all could use something to eat. Why don't I go into the kitchen and rustle up some sandwiches, and maybe some hot cocoa? It's gotten really chilly outside."

"Good idea, Pam," Marie said. "When your father finally comes home with the Thoros, he'll probably be hungry, too."

"Matt's still at Long Branch?" Dru asked, and Marie nodded. "Then he doesn't know about me?"

"No, he doesn't. He'll be pretty upset when he finds out," Marie said. "But he'll be very glad that you're back." She looked up at Pam. "Pam, maybe you ought to stop by the Fillies' bunkhouse just in case any of them are awake, and tell them that Dru's been found, and that Emily and Penny are here with us. I don't want them to worry."

Pam nodded and strode out the door.

Now there was nobody left in the room except Marie, Dru, Penny, and Emily. Marie removed some straw from Dru's hair and said gently, "I think it's time you talked to us, Dru. Tell us what happened."

"Well . . . " Dru rested her head against Marie's shoulder, looked over at Penny, and glanced away. "It's like this. I didn't want to come to Webster's. I didn't want to go anywhere this summer, but Mother and Daddy said we all had to go to camp. My sisters, Sarah and Eliza, are terrific gymnasts—they're both older than me, and they're really *beautiful*. They went to a gymnastics camp in the

Berkshires. And my brother Dave went to tennis camp. He's older than me, too. I'm the youngest . . . . "

Emily listened, fascinated. She'd never heard Dru talk so much since she'd known her.

" . . . and I'm the fattest, and the klutziest!" Dru sighed. "So I had a choice. I either had to go to one of those fat farms where you go to lose weight, or to someplace where I'd get lots of exercise and learn to be athletic like Sarah, Eliza, and Dave. Mother and Daddy decided I had to come here. I guess they thought it would be good for me, because . . . "

"Because why, Dru?" Marie asked, stroking Dru's hair.

"Because they thought I needed a wholesome family atmosphere, since we don't have one at home."

"What do you mean?" Penny asked.

"You really want to know?" Dru sat up and clasped her hands tightly in her lap. "My parents are getting a divorce. They've been married for eighteen years, and they're getting divorced! Sarah and Eliza and I live with Mother at the house, and Dave lives with Daddy in his apartment. And their lawyers are fighting about who gets custody of us kids. Daddy wants Dave, and Mother wants Sarah and Eliza, and neither of them wants *me*! I know they don't! I heard them arguing one day when I came home from school. Mother was saying that she can't handle three kids, and it wasn't fair for Dad to take

84

only one, and Daddy said he could take care of Dave all right, but he couldn't be responsible for any of the rest of us." Dru glanced at Emily. "That's what I meant when I told you I didn't have a home. I *don't*! Nobody wants me! Nobody cares about me. It'd make things a lot easier for everybody in my family if I just disappeared. So that's what I decided to do. I disappeared."

"Where did you disappear *to*?" Penny asked.

"Well, at first I thought I'd hide out in a cave or something. Only I didn't know where any caves were, so I thought maybe I'd just hide in the woods." Dru was really getting into her story now. For the first time in her life, she had a fascinated audience, and she was enjoying it. "It was kind of dark and scary under the trees, though. I didn't get very far. Then I thought about hiding in the boat house down by the river, so I went there. But it was scary there, too. And then I thought of hiding in the hayloft over the stables, but when I got there, there were lots of squeaky noises, like rats or something. So I went down to that place where you keep all the currycombs and stuff—"

"And that's where I found her!" Emily interrupted. "She was all bundled up in a lot of horse blankets, and I didn't see her, so I fell right on top of her."

She was sure that Marie was going to ask what she had been doing in the stable herself, but Marie didn't. Instead, she said, "Dru, I'm just so very glad

86

Emily found you. We don't want you to disappear, and I'm sure your parents don't, either. We all care about you a lot." She hugged Dru tightly, and Dru rested her head on Marie's shoulder.

"We sure do!" Penny said.

"My folks don't," Dru mumbled. "They don't care about me at all."

"I bet they do," Emily said. "I bet they care a lot more than you think. Did you ever tell them you didn't want to go to horse camp?"

"Nobody asked me," Dru said in a small voice.

"Did you tell them you were scared of horses?" Emily persisted.

"No . . . I didn't *know* I was scared of horses until I came here," Dru replied. "I didn't know much about horses at all. And then there they all were, and everybody was so crazy about them, and they're so *big*, and—"

"Snack time!"

Pam came into the room carrying a tray of sandwiches and mugs of hot chocolate. She set the tray down on the coffee table in front of the couch.

"There's peanut butter and jelly on Mom's homemade bread. The jelly's homemade, too," she said.

"Dig in, girls," Marie said. "I think I'll have one myself." She picked up a sandwich, and so did Penny and Emily.

But Dru shook her head. "I'm not very hungry. I think I'll just have some cocoa."

Emily, Penny, and Pam stared at her, amazed.

"Dru, are you feeling okay?" Penny asked anxiously.

"You're *always* hungry," Emily said.

"Not tonight." Dru heaved a huge sigh. "I don't think I'll ever be hungry again."

Just then, Emily heard the front door open and close. A moment later, Matt Webster appeared in the doorway.

"What's this? A nighttime picnic?" he asked, smiling at everyone. "Great! I'm starved!" His smile faded as he saw five solemn faces. He turned to Marie. "Something wrong?"

"Sit down, dear," Marie said. "One of our Fillies has a very big problem."

Chapter 8

While Matt ate the sandwich Dru didn't want, Marie told him everything that had happened. Dru just sat there, taking little sips from her mug of cocoa.

"Emily found her," Marie finished by saying. "She tripped over Dru in the stall where we keep the grooming equipment."

"What were you doing there?" Matt asked Emily, but he didn't sound angry at all—he just wanted information.

Emily took a deep breath. "I wanted to get a cloth to rub Joker down, because—because he was kind of sweaty under his saddle pad after I took him out without permission so I could help look for Dru," she said, all in a rush.

"I see." Matt nodded, and Marie and Pam looked surprised.

"Emily, you know it's against the rules to take your horse out—" Pam began.

"Without permission or supervision. Yes, I know." Emily stared down at her clasped hands. "But I was so worried about Dru . . . ."

"You *were*?" Dru said. "You were so worried about me that you did it anyway?"

"Yes, I was," Emily said. She couldn't bring herself to look at Matt, Marie, or Pam.

"Thanks, Emily," Dru said very softly. "I didn't think I wanted to be found, but I guess I really did."

"See? I *told* you we all care about you!" Penny said.

"Yes, Dru, we do," Matt added. "When you come to Webster's, you're part of our family, as I'm sure Marie has told you."

"Do you want to call your parents?" Marie asked. "Maybe not tonight, because it's pretty late, but in the morning?"

Dru thought about it for a few minutes, then said, "No, I don't think so. They'd just say I fouled up again, and they'd yell at me. Besides, my mother's on a cruise somewhere, and my dad's on vacation, too. I don't think they're back yet."

Matt stood up. "You know, Dru, I think the best thing for you to do right now is to go back to the bunkhouse and go to bed. Emily and Penny, too. We'll talk about everything in the morning, all right?"

Dru sighed. "Okay. I'm pretty tired. I didn't sleep

much all wrapped up in those horse blankets. They made my nose itch."

Pam stood up, too. "Let's go, Fillies!" she said briskly.

As Pam led Dru and Penny out of the room, Emily lagged behind. Looking from Matt to Marie, she said, "Will you tell me what my punishment is tomorrow?"

"For taking Joker out to look for Dru?" Marie said.

Emily nodded.

"I wouldn't worry about it, if I were you." Matt rested a hand on Emily's shoulder. "The next time the Fillies are on garden detail, maybe we'll ask you to weed out some of those baby carrots. I imagine Joker would enjoy them a lot."

"Then you're not going to take Joker away from me?"

"No way." Matt grinned at her. "Joker's your horse for the summer. I might have felt differently if you hadn't cared enough about him to want to rub him down. But you did, and because you did, you found Dru. Sleep tight, Emily."

Emily beamed. "Thanks, Matt!" She glanced over at Marie and added, "Thank you, too, Marie. Thanks for everything!"

She ran down the hall, hurrying to catch up with the others.

As they walked across the grass to the Fillies' bunkhouse, Pam said, "Things will look a lot brighter in the morning, Dru, believe me. And Sunday's the first camp horse show! That's always lots of fun—it's just for the campers, no outsiders, you know, and it's not really a competition, so you don't have anything to worry about. At the first show of the season, everybody demonstrates what they've learned during the first two weeks at Webster's, and you've learned a lot. You're a much better rider than you were when you first came."

"I couldn't ride *at all* when I first came," Dru reminded her.

"Yes, but now you can," Penny said eagerly. "I bet you've made more progress than any other camper."

But Dru shook her head. "I don't want to be in the horse show."

"Sure you do," Emily said. "It's going to be fun, like Pam said."

"Not for me. I'll just do something dumb, and then everybody will laugh at me." Dru heaved a huge sigh.

"No, you *won't* do something dumb, and nobody's going to laugh at you," Pam said. "Look, Dru, if you give us half a chance, we'll be your friends—*all* of us. But you have to meet us halfway."

They had reached the cabin now, and Pam put a finger to her lips. "Sssh—no more talking now. The rest of the Fillies are going to be real glad to see you in the morning, Dru, you'll see. They were all asleep when I came by earlier tonight, so I didn't tell them we'd found you. It'll be a super surprise!'' Pam whispered.

"See what I mean?'' Dru whispered back. "If they were *really* my friends, they would have stayed awake to find out if I was all right!''

"Do me a favor—just go to bed, okay?'' Pam sighed.

As the four of them tiptoed into the bunkhouse, Emily wondered if there was any way at all to make poor, sad Dru into a happy person. Somehow, she was beginning to doubt it.

Instead of waking up very early, the way she usually did, and making a morning visit to Joker before the rest of the campers were stirring, Emily slept late the next day, since she'd been up so late the night before. It was the excited voices of the other Fillies that finally made her open her eyes.

"Hey, Dru, you're back!'' Libby sang out from the upper bunk.

"Are you okay?'' Danny asked.

"Where'd you go?'' Lynda cried.

"I guess you weren't kidnapped after all,'' Caro said. "See? I told you so. Who'd want to kidnap *Dru?''* she added to nobody in particular.

"She's back, she's fine, and she didn't go very far,'' Pam told them. "And no, Caro, she wasn't kidnapped. I'm going to go brush my teeth. Come on, Fillies, get moving! Rise and shine!''

"Gee, Dru, weren't you scared, all alone out there

in the dark?" Danny said, stopping by Dru's bunk. "I'd have been terrified!"

"It was kind of scary," Dru admitted.

"Why did you do it?" Lynda asked. "I mean, were you running away?"

"No, she wasn't," Penny put in quickly. "She just wanted to—to be by herself for a while, right, Dru?"

Dru nodded.

"I can understand that," Caro said, much to Emily's surprise. "Sometimes it gets to be an awful drag being surrounded by people all the time. Especially people you never wanted to be surrounded by in the first place." That sounded more like Caro. "And I guess you must have figured that we'd all be mad at you for ruining our overnight trail ride. Well, you were absolutely right." Caro got out of her bunk and went over to the bathroom door, rapping on it sharply. "Pam? Aren't you finished brushing your teeth? It's my turn now."

Libby flung out her arms in an exaggerated gesture of comic despair. "It's always your turn! The rest of our teeth could decay and fall on the floor, and it would still be your turn!"

Caro gave her an icy look. "If you knew how much money my parents spent on my orthodontia, you'd know how important it is for me to take care of my teeth. I never miss a single day of FBI."

"FBI?" Danny repeated.

"Yes—Flossing, Brushing, and Irrigation."

Suddenly Caro and her expensive teeth had be-

94

come the focus of everyone's attention, and Dru's adventure was forgotten.

But not by Emily, and not by Penny or Dru herself. Dru would have curled back into her little blanket cocoon if Penny and Emily hadn't urged her to get up, get dressed, and go to breakfast at the farmhouse.

"Where's Dru?" Libby asked about an hour later. All the campers were busy cleaning out their horses' stalls before saddling up for riding class, and Libby had stopped by Joker's stall on her way to dump a wheelbarrow full of muck.

"She's probably still up at the house talking to Matt and Marie," Emily said. "It was too late last night and everybody was too tired to figure out what to do."

"How come you know so much about it?" Libby asked.

So Emily gave her a quick rundown on the events of the night before. When she'd finished, Libby said admiringly, "Wow! It must have been exciting! Why didn't you ask me to go with you?"

"By the time I made up my mind, you were asleep," Emily said. "And it was kind of exciting, but mostly it was sad. Dru doesn't want to stay here, but she doesn't have anywhere else to go. She really doesn't have a home, at least until her folks get back. And even then, she thinks they don't want her."

"Oh, for heaven's sake!" Caro's head popped up

in the stall next to Joker's where she was struggling with a pitchfork. "I am sick to death of hearing about poor, pitiful Dru. What's so tragic about having your parents park you in camp while they go on vacation? The same thing happened to me, and even though I'd much rather be in Europe than mucking out this messy stall, *I* don't sit around feeling sorry for myself all the time!"

"You know, Caro, you're right," Libby said. "I never realized it before, but you and Dru are kind of in the same boat, aren't you?"

"We are *not*!" Caro's pretty face flushed with anger. "*My* parents aren't getting divorced—and if they were, they'd both want me to live with them. It's not the same thing at all." She turned back to her work, muttering to Vic, "Move over, horse!"

Emily sighed. "If only Dru wasn't so scared of horses, maybe she'd forget about her problems at home for a while and have some fun."

"Yeah—maybe. But she is afraid, and I don't see that there's anything we can do about it," Libby said, picking up the handles of the wheelbarrow and starting off. "See you in a few," she called over her shoulder to Emily.

Emily was forking clean straw into Joker's stall when she heard Chris Webster's voice.

"How'd it go last night? Did you tell Mom and Dad that you took Joker out?" he asked, leaning on the stall door.

Emily looked up and smiled. "Everything's okay. I told Matt, and he wasn't mad or anything."

"That's good. I just came from the house. Mom and Dad just finished a long talk with Dru. I passed her on my way here."

"How did she look?" Emily asked.

Chris shrugged. "About the same, I guess. You know, I was thinking—Dru thinks nobody likes her, right?"

Emily nodded. "She doesn't even think her *horse* likes her, and she's so scared of Donna that she doesn't know her at all."

"I wonder . . ." Suddenly Chris's voice got a lot louder. "It's too bad about Donna. I'm getting real worried about her."

Puzzled, Emily said, "You are? Why? And why are you shouting?"

"I'm worried about her because I can tell she's not happy," Chris yelled. "See, I know all our horses real well, so I notice right away when something's wrong. And something's wrong with good old Donna. For one thing, she's off her feed."

"She is? But she's so plump. I thought she ate like a . . ."

Chris shook his head sadly. "She *used* to eat a lot, but she doesn't anymore. And I bet I know why."

"Chris, why are you talking so loud?" Caro asked, peering at him over the wall.

"*Sssh!*" Chris jerked his head in the direction of

97

the stable door. Both Emily and Caro looked and saw Dru standing about ten feet away from them.

"Oh, I get it," Caro said, and began grooming Vic.

Emily got it, too. "Why do you think Donna's off her feed?" she asked, raising her voice. She just hoped Dru could hear what they were saying over the other campers' voices and the occasional snorts and shuffles of the horses.

"She's off her feed because she's lonely and sad. Donna's a very sensitive mare. She knows when somebody doesn't like her, and Dru acts like she doesn't like her," Chris hollered.

"I don't think Dru doesn't like her," Emily shouted. "She's just scared of her. Dru's never been around horses before."

"Well, all I know is she's hurt Donna's feelings. I bet Donna's so sad she might even get sick. Dad might have to call the vet!"

"Oh, poor Donna! You don't think she's going to *die* or anything, do you?" Maybe that was laying it on a little thick, but Emily was really getting into it now.

"You never can tell," Chris said loudly. "It wouldn't take much to make her feel better. She just needs to know that the rider Dad assigned her to for the summer really *likes* her and isn't scared of her. If Dru was nice to her, made friends with her, she'd feel better right away."

Chris was facing Emily, so he couldn't see Dru

98

walking slowly, thoughtfully, past them, but Emily could. She watched as Dru stopped in front of Donna's stall. The little strawberry roan stuck her head out. Her ears were perked up, and she looked the picture of health, Emily noticed regretfully, not like a horse that was sorrowful and suffering. Emily held her breath. What would Dru do?

For a moment, Dru just stood there looking at Donna. Then she dug into her jeans pocket and took something out—it looked like the crumbled remains of a muffin. Dru held out the muffin on the palm of her hand, and Donna stretched out her neck, then delicately nibbled at the crumbs. As Chris turned around to watch, Dru flinched and almost pulled her hand away. But she didn't. Instead, she waited until every crumb was gone, and then she patted Donna's nose.

Chris turned back to Emily and grinned. "Who knows?" he whispered. "It's a start, anyway."

Caro had been watching, too, and now she said, "I have to admit that was a pretty clever idea, Chris. Maybe if Dru starts feeling sorry for Donna, she'll stop feeling so sorry for herself." She gave Chris one of her biggest, brightest smiles—the kind she usually reserved for Warren, Emily noticed with surprise. She couldn't help wondering what Caro was up to.

And she soon found out.

"Chris, I was wondering if you'd mind doing me just the tiniest little favor," Caro went on.

"Like what?" Chris asked.

"Well . . . I have all this nasty, dirty straw here in a big pile, and I know we're supposed to take it out into the stable yard, but I'm so awfully *clumsy* with a wheelbarrow. And yesterday, Vic stepped on my foot, remember? So I was wondering . . . "

"Okay, okay. I get the picture. I'll take care of it."

Before he walked away, Emily said softly, "It *was* a clever idea, Chris. Thanks a lot—I mean it. Maybe it'll work. Like you said, who knows?"

"No big deal. Let me know what happens, okay?"

"Chris, the *wheelbarrow,*" Caro whined. "Hurry up—please? I don't want to be late for class!"

"Yes, ma'am! One wheelbarrow, coming right up!"

Chris winked at Emily, then ambled away, doing an exaggerated, bowlegged cowboy walk. Emily giggled.

Chapter 9

Fifteen minutes later, Emily was in the intermediate ring with Penny, Danny, and the other members of her class—Carla, Karen, and Debby, who were Foals, and Meghan and Lisa, two Thoros.

"All right, girls, today and tomorrow we're going to be brushing up on everything we've learned so far, because we want to make a good showing on Sunday," Pam said, standing in the middle of the ring. "As you all know, Webster's has horse shows every two weeks, and the first one, the one this Sunday, is for campers only. You won't be competing for ribbons and trophies, so you don't have to worry about being better or worse than anybody else. The point of the first show of the season is to demonstrate how much you've learned." She grinned at them all. "I guess when you come right down to it, the only person who'll be on trial on Sunday is *me*!

If my riders don't look good, *I* don't look good, because I've taught you all you know."

"You mean, if we foul up, Matt and Marie will fire you?" Lisa teased.

"Yeah—they'll fire their very own daughter!" Karen called out, giggling.

"You got it!" Pam called back. "So you have to make me look *terrific.* I don't want to change my name from Webster to something else! Let's go, gang! We're going to walk, trot, and canter on command, and then we're going to jump. Meghan, lead off!"

Emily was right behind Meghan, and, as always, Joker responded to her signals beautifully. They didn't make a single mistake. Neither did Danny or Penny, or the rest of the group.

While she was waiting for Pam to set up the jumps, Emily stood up in her stirrups to see what was happening in the beginners' ring. So did Penny.

"Dru's doing really well," Penny said to Emily. "She got Donna on the right lead without any help from Rachel!"

"Maybe she's not as scared of Donna as she used to be," Emily said.

"Do you think she'll ride in the show after all?" Penny asked.

"I don't know. Possibly." Emily hadn't told Penny about her conversation with Chris. Nobody knew about that except Caro.

"Oh, I hope she will!" Penny cried. "If she's in

the show with the rest of us, then maybe she'll be happier. And I will, too," she added. "It's kind of hard trying to cheer Dru up all the time."

Emily nodded. "I know what you mean!"

"Hey, Emily, Penny. Break it up, will you?" Pam shouted. "This is a riding class, remember, not a pajama party. We're going to jump *without stirrups* this time. Penny, you follow Lisa, and Emily, you're next. Okay, Lisa—drop stirrups. Walk Tucker around the ring once, and when I say 'go,' take up the canter. Hands apart—that's the way. Legs, Lisa, *legs!* Hold him firmly with your *legs!* Good. Very good! You're doing just fine. All right, Lisa—go!"

Emily watched, tightening her grip on Joker's reins, as Lisa and Tucker approached the jump. Tucker took it without breaking stride, and though Lisa lurched a little in the saddle, she regained her seat and slowed him to a walk, stroking his shoulders and neck.

"Okay, Penny, your turn! Drop stirrups, walk . . ."

For the rest of the class, Emily didn't think about Dru at all. She didn't think about anything except doing her very best.

"Guess I'm not going to get fired after all," Pam said an hour and a half later. "You're the best group I've ever had!" She grinned at her proud students. "I bet you think I say that every summer. Well, you're right, but only because it's true. Each group seems to learn faster than the one before . . . ." She paused, then added, "Maybe that's because every year, I learn more, too, and become a better teacher. Or at least, I hope I do!" Pam hitched up her jeans and started for the gate. "Cool down your horses, gang. See you at lunch."

While Emily unsaddled Joker and rubbed him down, she kept an eye on Dru. She couldn't see a whole lot from Joker's stall, so she made several trips back and forth to pick up a different brush, or to return a currycomb, or to get a clean rubbing cloth. Every time she passed Donna's stall, she glanced in to see how Dru and Donna were getting along.

The first time, Dru was struggling to unbuckle Donna's girth, and Emily heard her say, "I hope I'm not hurting you, Donna. If you're off your feed like Chris said, maybe you have a stomachache. I'm kind of off my feed, too, I guess." Emily pretended that there was something wrong with one of her boots; she bent down and fiddled with it so she could hear more. "I only ate half a muffin at breakfast—I was going to save the rest for later, but I gave it to you instead. I hope you enjoyed it—it had blueberries in it," Dru went on. Emily thought Dru sounded as though she were making conversation with somebody she didn't know very well and was trying to be polite. And in a way, she was.

"What's the matter with your foot, Emily?" Lynda asked as she came out of Dan's stall. "Got a blister?"

"I thought so, but I don't think so," Emily replied. Then she realized how dumb that sounded and said, "I mean, I thought *maybe* I was getting a blister, but I'm not."

She hurried into the empty stall where she'd found Dru last night, grabbed a brush, and returned to Joker.

"Guess what, Joker," she said excitedly as she brushed his golden coat. "Dru's actually talking to Donna! Isn't that terrific?"

Joker made no comment, but Caro did.

"Wonderful," she said sarcastically. "And next you're going to say that Donna answered her."

"No, she didn't. But I bet she appreciated having Dru pay attention to her for a change."

Suddenly Emily realized that for the first time since the "big fight," Caro had spoken directly to her. It made her feel good. Emily had never made anybody so mad at her that they wouldn't talk to her before, and even though she didn't like Caro much, she was glad that Caro had finally recognized her existence once again.

Caro didn't say anything else—she was too busy grooming Vic, or at least she seemed to be.

On Emily's second trip past Donna's stall she walked very slowly and heard Dru saying, "You're not going to step on me or anything, are you, Donna? I'm just trying to brush your hair . . . uh . . . your mane. It's kind of tangled. My hair gets that way sometimes. I hate it when I run the comb through and it pulls. I really don't want to hurt you, honest I don't. And I don't know about your tail . . . . I guess I should comb that, too, but you might not like it, and I'm afraid you might . . . well, kick me or something. So we'll forget about your tail for now, okay?"

On the third trip, Emily saw that Rachel was standing by the door of Donna's stall, speaking to Dru. Emily paused by the stall next to Donna's to pat the nose of one of the Foals' ponies—and to eavesdrop. She couldn't help herself!

"Dru, I'm really pleased with the way you handled Donna this morning," Rachel was saying. "You were the best one in the beginners' class."

"Was I? You're not just saying that to make me feel good, are you?"

"Come on, Dru! You know me better than that—or you should. I don't hand out compliments unless I mean them. Why should I tell you how good you were if you *weren't* good, know what I mean? You didn't hold onto the saddle once. I know you're going to be my star pupil in the horse show on Sunday!"

"The horse show . . . " Dru's voice faded away.

"Yes, the horse show. I'm counting on you, Dru."

"Am I . . . do you think I'm . . . well, better than Ellen?" Dru asked. Ellen was the only Thoroughbred in the beginners' class, and she was three years older than Dru.

"You've made a lot more progress than Ellen has," Rachel told her. "She's still kind of awkward—she hasn't established any communication with her horse yet. And you hadn't either, until today. This morning, I got the feeling that you and Donna were on the same wavelength for the first time. It was like you weren't scared of Donna anymore."

Emily stroked the pony's neck, straining to hear what Dru had to say.

"I'm not *as* scared," Dru mumbled. "Not since I found out that Donna might get sick and die because she thinks I don't care about her. I didn't know horses felt that way. I thought only people did. But I heard Chris talking to Emily, and he said . . . "

"What did Chris say? I'm all ears," Rachel said.

Emily decided it was time to step in. "He told *me* how sad Donna was because she thought Dru didn't like her. He said Donna's not eating right because she's so unhappy," Emily said quickly.

Rachel stared at her in amazement. *"Donna?* Not *eating?"*

"Yes—because she's so sad. Chris said Donna's been kind of pining away. She's a very sensitive horse and she can tell when somebody doesn't like her, especially when the person is going to be riding her for the whole summer." Emily turned to Dru. "You heard him, didn't you, Dru?"

"Yes, I did." Dru nodded solemnly. "That's what he said, all right. And it really made me feel bad, because it's not that I don't *like* Donna. I like her better than any other horse at Webster's. But I *was* scared of her. I guess I still am, a little. But not as much. And I'm going to try to make it up to her, because I didn't mean to hurt her feelings. It's awful to think nobody cares about you," she added softly.

Emily met Rachel's eyes for a moment and returned the older girl's smile.

Rachel reached out and patted Donna, who had ambled over to find out what was going on. "You know, Dru," she said, "Chris was absolutely right. Donna hasn't been looking as happy as she used to, and I've been wondering why. Now I know—and so do you. And you know what's going to make her feel just fine?"

"No. What?"

"Having you ride her in the horse show on Sunday. If you don't, she'll think it's because you're still scared of her and you don't really like her at all. All the other horses will be out there in the ring, and Donna will be all by herself in the stable. That'll make her miserable—kind of the way you'd feel if everybody else was having a good time and you weren't included. And you don't want her to feel that way, do you?"

Dru shook her head. "No. No, I don't."

"Then you're going to be in the show, right?"

Dru smiled a little. "Right!"

"Great!" Rachel gave Donna another pat, then left, whistling between her teeth.

Emily looked at her wristwatch. "Gee, it's almost time for lunch. I'm starved! How about you, Dru?"

"In a minute. I think I ought to stay with Donna a little longer," Dru said. "I don't want her to think I'm deserting her or anything. After all, she depends on me. I guess I'm just about her best friend."

Emily headed back to Joker's stall, grinning from ear to ear.

Chapter 10

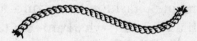

After lunch—macaroni and cheese, lots of home-grown salad, and plenty of ice-cold milk, topped off with chocolate chip cookies—Emily asked Penny to take Dru to visit the mares and foals during rest period.

"What if she doesn't want to go?" Penny asked.

"Talk her into it," Emily said firmly. "You can do it. And while you're both gone, I'm going to make the rest of the Fillies see that we all have to help Dru come out of her shell. She's already started just a little bit, but we need to show her that we're behind her all the way."

"How are you going to do that?" Penny wanted to know.

"I have a plan," Emily said. "Just make sure she's gone for about half an hour, okay?"

"Okay. I'll do it."

Penny trotted off, calling, "Hey, Dru, wait up!"

Emily headed for the Fillies' bunkhouse. She *did* have a plan. She just hoped it would work.

In the Fillies' cabin, Libby was polishing her boots, Lynda was writing a letter to her family back in Iowa, Danny was lying on her stomach in her bunk reading *National Velvet* for the fourteenth time, and Caro was peering into the mirror above the bureau, looking at a fashion magazine and experimenting with a new hairstyle. Pam had taken off for her daily ride on Firefly. It was very hot—the sun that had refused to shine on the Fillies' trail ride was now beating down on the roof—and not even the electric fan on the windowsill provided much comfort.

Emily paused on the threshold, gathering her courage. She didn't think she'd have much trouble convincing Libby, Lynda, and Danny to help Dru, but Caro was a different story. And Caro was a very important part of her plan.

"Hey, guys," Emily said loudly, entering the cabin, "I think it's time we talked about Dru."

"So talk," Libby said cheerfully.

"Not just me. *All* of us," Emily said.

"What are we supposed to talk about?" Lynda asked. "She ran away, and now she's back."

"Velvet's riding The Pie in the Grand National at

Aintree," Danny murmured, as though she'd never read the book before. "Nobody knows she's a girl!"

"I don't really like banana clips," Caro said, examining her reflection in the mirror. "Everybody's wearing them. I think maybe I'm going to buy one of those crimper things. I bet my hair would look fantastic all wiggly like that . . . ."

Emily stamped her foot, and everybody looked up, startled.

"I don't *care* about any of that stuff!" she cried. "I care about Dru. She's agreed to ride in the show on Sunday, and that's terrific, but she still needs a lot of support from her friends, or else she's going to be unhappy again." Now that she'd gotten everyone's attention, Emily lowered her voice. "We have to make Dru feel really good about herself. And that means that we have to show her that we care about *her,* because she's a Filly just like us. And she has a lot more problems than the rest of us do."

"You mean because she's fat and wears braces and is scared of horses?" Caro asked. "She's got problems, all right!"

"It's much worse than that," Emily said. "Dru's folks are getting a divorce, and she thinks neither of them wants her to live with them. She thinks they both like her brother and sisters better than her."

"Wow! That's rough," Lynda said softly. "No wonder she's so sad all the time."

Danny put down her book. "If *my* parents were getting divorced, I think I'd cry day and night!"

"What do you want us to do, Emily?" Libby asked.

"Yes, what?" Caro added. "We can't make her mother and father get back together again. And if they don't like her, there's nothing we can do about that, either." She flipped over another page in her magazine. "Maybe I should try a perm . . . . "

"I said we have to make Dru feel good about herself, and that's what I meant," Emily said stubbornly. "I know we can't do anything about the divorce, but if Dru stops thinking she's so fat and ugly that her parents can't possibly love her, and that *we* don't like her, either, maybe she'll start feeling better. And if Dru starts feeling better, we will, too. Know what I mean?"

"It *would* be nice not to have her moping around for a change," Caro agreed. She turned over another page. "Now look at this girl. She's not a model or anything—she was just a plain, dumpy teenager like Dru. Or like Dru will be when she gets a little older, if she doesn't shape up. *This* girl . . . " she shoved the magazine under Emily's nose " . . . had a complete makeover! She lost about twenty pounds, and she learned how to style her hair and wear the right clothes, and she turned out pretty well. Look at the 'before' and 'after' pictures."

Danny couldn't see the pictures, but she said eagerly, "Just like the girl in *My Fair Lady*! Do you think we could turn Dru into a beautiful princess?"

Caro's big, beautiful eyes lit up. "Maybe not a

beautiful princess, but with a little help, she could look better than she does now . . . . "

"I'm not just talking about looks," Emily interrupted. "What I'm saying is, let's show Dru that she's a valuable person."

"Dru's okay, really," Lynda said. "I don't know her very well—as a matter of fact, I don't know her at all, I guess—but I'll do whatever I can to make her happy here at Webster's."

"Me, too," Libby added. "Maybe I could give her a few pointers on handling Donna. Not that Donna needs much handling—she was the first horse I ever rode at Webster's, and she has the sweetest disposition."

"I wonder if she's ever read *National Velvet*," Danny said. "I'll lend her my copy, if she promises to be very careful with it and read every single word!"

Caro was flipping through her magazine, frowning intently. "Maybe a banana clip wouldn't look too silly on Dru. She has kind of mousy hair, but if I played around with it . . . "

Emily glanced out one of the windows and saw Penny and Dru trudging toward the Fillies' bunkhouse. They were talking animatedly, and Dru didn't look unhappy at all.

"They're coming," she said. "Don't overdo it, okay? If Dru thinks we're doing a number on her, she'll only feel worse. Remember, she's just one of us Fillies. And Fillies stick together, don't we?"

"There's this diet on page ninety-six," Caro murmured. "Lots of fruits and vegetables. You can even have a muffin every day, if you don't drown it in butter. As for eggs . . . "

"It's time for the beginners' class," Penny whispered to Emily on Sunday afternoon. "Look—Rachel's leading them into the ring!"

Emily, wearing her only good pair of riding breeches, was leaning over the fence that surrounded the advanced ring where the horse shows were always held. Her brown wavy hair was concealed by her velvet hard hat, and her boots gleamed from the polishing she'd given them the night before. The sun was beating down on the beautiful countryside, and the distant Adirondacks formed a greenish-purple background to the entire scene.

"Dru's looking good," Emily whispered back. "She's not acting scared at all."

"She's not—not anymore." Penny rested her chin on her folded arms as she leaned over the top of the white rail fence. "She looks thinner, too, don't you think?"

Emily had to admit that Dru *did* look thinner, though it hardly seemed possible that only two days of careful dieting could have produced such an immediate effect.

"Look, they're starting off!" Penny breathed.

One by one, the members of the beginners' class

116

were riding around the ring under the watchful eye of Matt Webster, who stood in the center of them holding a clipboard.

"Trot!" Matt commanded, and the young riders trotted, keeping a careful distance between themselves and the next horse and rider in line. Dru and Donna were right behind a Foal on her pinto pony. The Foal bounced in the saddle, her expression grim as she tried to hold her reins while posting to the rhythm of her pony's gait. Dru raised and lowered herself in the saddle, keeping her eyes focused between Donna's ears. Emily could see her lips moving as she spoke to her mount. And when Donna tossed her head, Dru didn't flinch or grab for the pommel.

Lynda and Danny joined Emily and Penny as Dru's class began to canter.

"Go, Dru, go!" Libby yelled from where she was perched on the top rail of the fence a little farther away. Dru glanced her way and gave her a brief grin.

"She smiled! Dru actually *smiled*," Lynda said. "I can't believe it!"

"I think she's the very best one," Penny said happily.

Now Rachel came into the ring and went over to Matt. She handed him something—Emily couldn't see what it was—and looked at the notes he was making on his clipboard.

"Guess Dad won't have to send for the vet after all," Chris said, keeping a straight face as he hooked his arms over the fence next to Emily. "I was real worried there for a while, though."

"Yes, I know," Emily said, equally solemn. "And so was Dru."

"But she's not anymore," Penny added. "She says all Donna needed was a little love."

"We all need that," Danny said softly.

As Matt put the riders through the rest of their paces, Dru rode Donna right past where they were standing.

"Dru looks different somehow," Chris said, frowning.

"Thinner?" Penny suggested.

"Happier?" Danny asked.

Chris shook his head. "That's not it . . . . " He thought for a minute. "Her eyes! That's what it is. She's got blue stuff on her eyes."

"For your information, Chris," Caro said, sauntering over from where she had been standing with the Thoros, "that 'blue stuff' happens to be my most *expensive* hypo-allergenic pearlescent eyeshadow, 'Silver Lagoon.' And she's also wearing just a touch of my 'Raspberry Parfait' transparent lip gloss with a sun protection factor of thirty-two. I think it makes her look lots older—more like a Filly and less like a Foal. I fixed her hair, too, but you can't see it under her hat." She sighed. "It's probably a mess by now. I definitely think she needs a perm. Maybe just a body wave . . . . "

"Sorry I mentioned it," Chris mumbled. He met

Emily's eyes, and they both suppressed snorts of laughter.

"Quiet! Listen!" Penny said excitedly. "Matt's making an announcement."

The riders had lined up with their mounts head to tail in the center of the ring. Matt called out, "As you all know, Webster's first show of the season isn't a competition, so we don't award prizes. This show gives all of us a chance to see what the other classes are doing, and how much they've learned during their first two weeks at camp. And I don't know about you, but I'm very impressed with how well Rachel's beginners' class has performed today. Let's give them all a hand!"

Everybody applauded, and Libby let out a piercing whistle that hurt Emily's ears.

"Now, before the intermediate class comes into the ring, there's just one more thing I have to say," Matt continued when the noise died down. "I said we don't give out awards at this show, and usually we don't. But this year, Rachel, Marie, and I felt that the rider in the beginners' class who has made the most progress deserves special recognition. So Marie made a very special ribbon, which I am about to present." He held up a big red, white, and blue rosette. Its bright streamers fluttered in the afternoon breeze.

Penny clutched Emily's arm. "Do you think . . . ?" she whispered.

Emily grinned. "I wouldn't be at all surprised!"

119

Matt handed the ribbon to Rachel. "On second thought, you make the award, Rachel—it's your class."

Rachel stepped forward, beaming. "The most improved rider in the beginners' class at Webster's Country Horse Camp is . . . "

Penny's fingers dug into Emily's arm. "I can't stand it!" she said.

" . . . a girl who was so terrified of horses when she first came here that she could hardly bear to look at one, much less ride one . . . . "

"Oh, come *on,* Rachel!" Caro sighed. "We'll be here all day!"

" . . . A girl who, in spite of all that, has learned to overcome her fears and to ride as well as any other girl in her class. Her progress in just the past couple of days has been fantastic . . . . "

"Hey, Rachel!" Libby shouted. "Like my grandmother says, cut the cackle and get to the eggs!"

Everybody laughed, including Rachel. "Okay, here goes. I'm proud to present Webster's first Most Improved Rider Award to Dru Carpenter!"

The Thoros applauded politely, but the Fillies, Chris, Marie, and Pam clapped until their hands were sore. Chris and Libby let out triumphant whoops.

"She won! Dru won! It's the first thing she's ever won in her whole life!" Penny shouted, jumping up and down.

Dru's round face was beet red with pride and embarrassment as she walked Donna over to where Rachel stood. With great ceremony, Rachel fastened the rosette to Donna's bridle.

"Congratulations, Dru," she said, patting Donna's sleek shoulder.

"Th-thank you, Rachel," Dru murmured. She leaned down and patted Donna, too. Then she sat up very straight in the saddle and said much more loudly, "I couldn't have gotten so much better if it wasn't for Donna—or without the help of my friends." She looked over at the Fillies, smiling broadly. Her braces glittered in the sunlight.

"Okay, Pam, get your class together. Intermediates next," Matt called as the beginners, Dru in the lead, rode out of the ring.

"Emily, Penny, that's us!" Danny cried.

"I have to see Dru first," Penny said, running off to congratulate her friend.

Before Emily hurried over to Joker, who was tethered with the rest of the horses under the trees nearby, she grinned at Chris. "You deserve a prize, too," she said.

"For what? Webster's Best Liar?" he replied, grinning back.

Emily laughed. "I know what your prize will be! We'll make you an honorary Filly!"

"Give me a break!" Chris groaned.

As Emily untied Joker and swung up into the sad-

dle, she was still smiling. She could hardly wait to write to Judy and tell her everything that had happened over the past few days. It was going to be a *very* long letter . . . .

Field Day is coming at Webster's Country Horse Camp, and Emily and her friends are determined to beat the boys from Camp Long Branch at horsemanship, softball, and swimming. They want to make a good showing in the Costume Parade, too. But Emily is miserable. She has no idea what her costume will be, and the girls can't seem to do anything but argue with each other. Can *anyone* make the campers into a team? And will Emily find the perfect costume before it's too late?

Don't miss HORSE CRAZY #3
Good Sports by Virginia Vail